bluewing

Other books by Kate Avery Ellison

The Curse Girl

Once Upon a Beanstalk

Frost (The Frost Chronicles #1)

Thorns (The Frost Chronicles #2)

Weavers (The Frost Chronicles #3)

bluewing

KATE AVERY ELLISON

ISBN-10: 1484842413

ISBN-13: 978-1484842416

For Paul and Sam

BLUEWING: THE FROST CHRONICLES #4

Lia Weaver is a fugitive. Her family's farm has been confiscated by Farther soldiers, her sister has been reassigned to a new family in the village, and her official status is "missing." Now, Lia and a band of fugitive followers must make their home in the harsh wilderness of the Frost. Food is scarce, and hope is scarcer still as Lia tries to find information about the whereabouts of her missing friends. She is determined to rescue them, but when a surprising ally steps forth with an offer that will both return her friends and expel the Farthers from the Frost in exchange for something precious, Lia must make a choice.

ONE

DARKNESS CLOTHED ME. Branches scratched my face. The wind tugged at tendrils of my hair that hung around my face. Somewhere to my left, an owl hooted.

Gabe moved beside me, his breathing loud in the stillness. His feet were clumsier than mine on the rocks, but he kept up with me as we slipped through the trees. A few paces behind us, a dark-haired fugitive named Arla followed. She matched Gabe for clumsiness, but she made no noise even when she stumbled and scraped her knee on a riverbed rock. But that didn't surprise me— she had scars on her arms and back where she'd been beaten by Farther soldiers before she'd escaped an Aerialian prison. I knew she was strong.

As we crested the final hill, I threw out a hand, signaling them both to stop. Below us, snow-lined roofs sparkled in the light of the moon, and the metal of the Farther gates and walls around them gleamed like a row of knives.

Iceliss.

I unfastened my cloak and rolled it into a ball to store at the roots of one of the trees. Gabe copied my movements. The night air stole my warmth, but now I was free to move without hindrance. I wore a black shirt and trousers like a boy, my long hair was caught up in braids and tucked beneath a hat, and a dark scarf obscured my nose and mouth. If anyone saw me, they wouldn't recognize me. Nothing I wore identified me as a Weaver, or even as a female. I was as anonymous as the night.

"Stay here," I murmured to Arla. "We'll be back soon."

We'd returned to the Frost only two weeks ago, and when we'd arrived, I'd discovered that my friends, Adam Brewer and Ann Mayor, were both gone. Adam had been arrested for his involvement with the Thorns, and Ann was being held somewhere in Astralux, accused of the same thing. I didn't know where either one of them was, but I was determined to find out.

Arla chafed her hands together for warmth as she stepped back into the shadow of the trees, and together Gabe and I crept toward the town.

A guard paced the length of the wall before us, and I could see the ugly shape of his gun by the faint light of the moon and stars. We skulked past him toward the artisans' quarter of the village where, we'd been told, there was a place where we could safely cross in and out of the town without detection from the soldiers.

I spotted the place where shadows pooled at the corner of the wall, making it too dark to see clearly from the top. The rise and intersection of three oddly shaped roofs blocked us from any soldier's view, just as Ivy had described.

As we watched, the soldier disappeared from sight.

My heart pounded in my chest, and my lungs ached with every shallow breath I took. Every sense in my body strained to detect a hint of danger. I raised a hand to signal to Gabe, and he nodded to show he'd seen.

We ran together across the narrow boundary of open ground between the trees and the wall, and the sound of our crossing was as loud as a shout to my ears. We reached the wall and pressed against it, looking up to see if we'd been seen.

We hadn't.

I held my breath as I slipped through the widest slit in the metal crossings. My hips scraped steel, but I wriggled through. A chill slid down my skin as my feet touched cobblestones on the other side. Gabe followed.

We were inside the village.

The slightest hiss of breath made me freeze. I looked—the soldier on the wall had returned. His body was an outline against the night sky, black shadow against almost black. I saw his rifle move, and my heart stuttered. Shivers slid down my arms. I went still as a dead rabbit.

The soldier continued on without stopping, and Gabe and I exhaled as one.

We didn't speak, but I nodded to show I was ready to continue. We moved house by house through the artisans' quarter and toward the center of the village. Every street was empty, a consequence of Officer Raine's curfew that he'd imposed on the entire community. Nothing stirred except us and the wind.

Gabe stumbled in the dark of an alley. He put his hand against a stack of small barrels lining the wall to steady himself.

"Careful," I whispered, because the barrels were piled precariously and looked almost ready to fall.

We crept through the market, which stood empty in the darkness, the banners fluttering halfheartedly in the wind and the stalls standing bare. We passed the base of the hill crowned by the Mayor's house, and I didn't turn my head to look, because looking at it only sent a stab of

11

pain straight to my heart. We passed the Quota Yard, the Meeting House, and finally, we reached the place we sought.

The Farther offices.

The building gleamed unnaturally in the moonlight, crouched between two buildings of stone, an ugly metal interloper amid the ancient architecture. I stole around the side, taking care not to make any noise that might alert the soldiers dozing at the front. Ivy had given us explicit instructions about how we might enter. At the back, a rain barrel sat just below a narrow window. The glass gleamed like ice.

Gabe held out one hand to steady me as I climbed from the barrel to the lip of the windowpane. I pressed my fingers to the glass. The seams creaked, and I froze, counting my breaths, waiting for soldiers to come running.

No one came.

I produced the tools I needed from my belt and began stripping away the paste that held the glass in place. It was a narrow opening, probably deemed too small to be a security concern, but I would be able to squeeze through. Near starvation had its benefits after all, I supposed.

The glass finally gave, and I passed the sheet down to Gabe before swinging my legs up and twisting my body to fit inside. The edges of the window scraped a layer of skin from my arms, but then I was free and I dropped to the floor below.

All was still quiet.

I reached into the pouch at my belt and produced a few of the glowing fungi that grew in the deepest regions of the Frost. Their faint light illuminated a desk, a chair, and a row of cabinets. I was in Korr's office. The same room he'd once interrogated me about Echlos' location.

I crossed the floor to the desk and fumbled with the drawers. My fingers brushed over papers—arrest records, prisoner processing documents. I ran my thumb down the names. A...B...

Brewer.

I pulled the papers from the drawer and set them on the desk before returning to the file. I looked under M, for Mayor, but there was nothing.

Ann was not recorded as being arrested for anything.

I muttered a curse and shut the drawer. There must be some record of where she'd gone, what had happened to her.

A faint rasp reached my ears from outside, the whisper of a foot against stone, and the urgency of what I was doing spurred me to action. I gathered up the papers for Adam and stuffed them into my belt. Lifting the glowing fungi, I crossed to the other side of the room to scan the shelves. I didn't know what I was looking for—anything that might give me a clue, I supposed. I saw books, a case of knives, the map of the Frost. A knife was embedded in the center of the map. Goose bumps rippled over my skin when I realized the point pierced the location of my family's farm.

Footsteps sounded in the hall. I dropped the fungi back into the pouch at my belt and scurried for the window. I hoisted myself up onto the sill with the aid of a chair and wriggled out, gasping at the pain as I forced myself through the tiny space once more. Then I was out, crouched on the window ledge, and Gabe was handing me the plate of glass, the whites of his eyes visible in the darkness. I wedged it against the frame, close enough to not be noticed, and then I scrambled down with Gabe's help.

As soon as my feet touched the cobbled stones of the alley below, I was already running. Gabe kept pace beside me, and we didn't stop until we'd passed the Meeting House and the walls of the Quota Yard. We caught our breath in a shadow below the new Farther clock tower.

"Did you get it?" he demanded, the first words he'd spoken since we'd left Echlos an hour ago.

I jerked my head in a nod even as my chest tightened at my failure to find everything. "I found Adam's file. There was nothing for Ann."

The admission filled me with despair. Gabe opened his mouth to reply, but there was a shout behind us.

"You there! Stop!"

We ran.

Lights flared, and we were flying over the cobblestones and through the darkness on unsteady legs. My heart pounded against my ribs as our pursuers drew closer. We couldn't outrun them. We had to hide.

Gabe pulled me behind a stack of firewood, and the soldiers ran past.

We stayed there, wedged between wood and stone for what felt like an eternity, the seconds and minutes measured by my heartbeat. Slowly, my panic eased. The wind whistled between the cracks in the wood. A mouse scratched in the wall behind us. Gabe's breath was soft against my shoulder.

When all had been silent for some time, we moved again.

The scuff of footsteps tore through the silence. A shout rang out. They'd been waiting for us to move.

There was no time to think, only to act. We needed an explanation for why we were out in the darkness. I grabbed the lapels of Gabe's shirt and pulled him close for a kiss. His lips parted under mine in surprise.

14

A light flared, illuminating our bodies, blinding me, and I heard the click of a gun.

"Don't move," a voice snarled.

We were trapped. There was nowhere to run. Slowly, I released Gabe's shirt.

They approached us, congealing into human form out of the darkness like nightmares. The tallest one stepped in front of us and ripped away my scarf. His expression didn't change; he didn't recognize me. Of course not. I was just one face among hundreds of villagers that he probably never glanced twice at.

"You've broken curfew," he said, glaring into my eyes. His gaze slid to Gabe, who was adjusting his scarf to cover his face again after our kiss.

Sweat prickled across my back. If the soldier removed Gabe's scarf, all would be lost, because Gabe resembled his brother, Korr, almost identically. The soldiers would recognize his face immediately, and they would know we were not ordinary villagers out for a midnight rendezvous.

The soldier reached up to tear the scarf away.

"I'm sorry," I stuttered out, desperate to distract him. "We didn't mean to—"

The soldier swung around to address me. "You people never do. A more inept bunch of backwater hicks, I've never encountered."

Rage curled in my stomach along with my fear, but I pushed it away. "Haven't you ever been in love?"

The soldier laughed in derision.

I didn't say anything else. I reached for Gabe's hand. Maybe he would think that's all we were, two foolish youngsters sneaking out past curfew to steal kisses.

Gabe's scarf forgotten, the soldier crossed his arms and eyed us both.

"Come," he commanded. "A flogging and a night in a cell will teach you to remember curfew next time."

Gabe and I exchanged a glance. We stepped away from the wall. My heart thudded in triple-time.

We needed to get out of here.

We came easily, docile, and the soldiers relaxed. They were tired; it was late. I could see them checking the path of the moon, muttering about their bunks. They weren't paying close attention, not when it came to a pair of village brats destined for a night in a cell to teach them a lesson about the foolishness of romance in the middle of a war.

We reached the main street. Ahead was the dark alley we'd come through before, the one lined with precarious stacks of barrels...barrels that might be easily dislodged.

I squeezed Gabe's hand to get his attention. I looked at the alley and nodded.

Now.

We ran. The soldiers shouted. When we reached the end of the alley, I whirled and shoved at the base of the stack of barrels. The whole wall of them crumbled behind us.

We turned the corner and scurried like rats down another alley. The soldiers stumbled over the fallen barrels in the dark, their shouts growing fainter, but we weren't out of danger yet. We reached the place where we'd entered the wall. I counted down with my fingers, and then we ran together, squeezing through the opening and slipping away into the night.

The Frost reached out cold arms to embrace us, and when we reached the trees I could finally breathe again. Every inch of my body felt scraped, sore, or numb. I tugged off the scarf covering my face and shook down my hair. Arla appeared from the darkness without a word. She took in our shaken expressions and bit her lip, then went to retrieve our cloaks.

"Are you all right?" I asked Gabe.

"I—I think so," he said. His voice shook. "You? That was quick thinking back there."

"I'm all right, too," I managed. Shock at our almost-capture numbed me, and beneath it, disappointment at my failure to find everything I'd been looking for throbbed like a new wound. I hadn't found anything about Ann.

I paused and wrenched the papers I'd taken from Korr's drawer from my belt. Holding them up to the moonlight, I squinted to make out the scribbled words. Each phrase sunk like a barb into my heart. *Arrest. Treason. Detainment facility. Astralux.* Slowly, I lowered my hands to my sides.

Astralux was so far away.

Folding the paper, I slipped it back into the bag at my belt and took a deep breath. I didn't mention the kiss back in the village, and Gabe didn't bring it up either. Since we'd retuned through the gate and I'd discovered that Adam had been captured, we hadn't been romantic. It was as if something inside me had gone cold. Gabe hadn't pressed the matter. Since his friend Claire's betrayal of us and subsequent disappearance, he had been quiet and withdrawn, too.

Arla handed me my cloak. I accepted it and threw the heavy cloth around my shoulders, and beside me, Gabe did the same. His expression, barely visible in the moonlight, was sympathetic. If anyone understood my anxiety and sorrow over my missing friends, he did. He'd lost almost his entire family. He didn't know if they were dead or alive. The quiet solidarity of our shared pain flowed between us, and I sighed.

"Let's go," I said.

We traveled as fast as possible in the dark, sticking to the shadowed places where the snow was lightest, taking care not to leave evidence of our passage as we wove through the labyrinth of unmarked trails and deer paths that led to our destination. And as my panic faded, I realized that for the first time in my life, I moved through the Frost unadorned by the blue blossoms that I'd always worn to keep away the monsters, because I knew a secret about myself now.

I, Lia Weaver, was the descendent of the creator of the Watchers.

They were not living creatures, but mechanical beasts designed to be sentient and almost indestructible. They were created with an insatiable desire to protect Echlos and the former ruins of the Compound, the place that had become the Frost after the end of that world and the beginning of this new one. And these beasts were created with a failsafe. They would not attack the descendants of their creator, not if they got a whiff of their blood.

I hadn't told anyone besides my siblings and Gabe yet, because I wasn't sure what it meant, or what anyone else would think. Recently, the Watchers had slain two Thorns operatives—Jacob, the leader of the fugitives from the Compound, and Atticus, leader of the Thorns operatives in the Frost. The pall of their deaths still lingered in everyone's minds.

Gabe scanned the trees. A vein throbbed in his throat, and his hands moved restlessly as he tugged at the snow blossoms he still wore around his neck for protection. Arla did the same.

"Any sign of Watchers?" she whispered. She'd never seen the monsters, but she'd heard the stories.

I shook my head. There was no hint of the blood-red glow of their eyes, no sound of their claws against the

18

ice. But that meant little. Watchers could move like ghosts through the night. Gabe and I both knew from experience.

After almost an hour of stumbles and hissed exclamations and ragged breaths drawn in darkness, we reached the top of a hill, and the shimmer of the ruins of Echlos greeted us.

Arla let out a sigh of relief. "We made it."

Just then, a cry split the night. I jerked around. Arla shrieked. Gabe's hand went to the snow blossoms at his throat.

"Watchers."

They must have been following us.

"Leave me here and go," I said.

"What are you going to do?" Arla's eyes were wide with terror.

I needed to try this. I hadn't done it since we'd returned and I needed to see that it would still work.

"Go." I pushed them both toward the ruins. "Don't stay. Don't look back. Just run."

"Lia—"

"Go now!"

Arla ran. Gabe stopped, and I gave him a glare. He did what I said without further hesitation as I yanked a knife from my belt. The blade almost slipped from my hands, they were trembling so hard, but I caught it and drew it across my finger without hesitation. Red beaded across my skin and fell to the snow as the creature burst from the trees.

It was a big one. Powerful haunches dug into the ground as the head swiveled to look at me. Spines bristled down its back, and its teeth glittered as it opened its mouth to emit a high-pitched cry.

I held my ground, drew in a deep breath, and stretched out my hand. Every inch of my skin prickled

19

with terror and excitement mingled together. Wind whipped my hair and snagged my cloak, flinging the fabric out as it carried my scent toward the Watcher.

The beast stiffened as it caught the smell of my blood. It stopped. It regarded me but did not charge. The jaws opened and closed, and the eyes dimmed. With a growl, the creature spun around and slunk back into the forest. The shadows rippled, and then it was gone, leaving only churned snow behind.

I exhaled as my whole body slumped in relief. Turning, I headed toward Echlos.

TWO

GABE GRABBED ME as soon as I ducked inside the darkness of the ruins. "Are you insane?" he demanded, giving my shoulders a shake. "You're not invincible, you know."

Beside him, Arla stood silent and trembling, her face the color of bleached bone.

"The Watcher is gone, and we're late," I said. "Come on. Let's get below before Jonn starts to worry."

"You're sure it's gone?" Gabe glanced at the entrance. The Watchers could enter Echlos. The walls did not keep them out. We had to use supreme caution when moving through the ruins at night.

"I'm sure," I said, and exhaustion washed over me. I started down the hallway, my boots thudding quietly, and they followed.

We descended the staircases into the depths of the Echlos ruins. Every so often, we passed a painted mural of a blue flower with five petals—a snow blossom. These were new additions. All the debris and dust was swept away wherever they appeared. We'd made them ourselves, because the drawings kept the Watchers at bay.

When we finally reached the bottom level, the door hissed open and a figure darted down the hall toward us.

I caught a glimpse of curly hair and an upturned nose—Everiss Dyer, another fugitive and former village resident. Her strained expression softened with relief as she saw it was us. Arla slipped past her into the main living area, leaving Everiss alone with Gabe and me.

Everiss and I had once been what most people would consider friends, although we'd never been close. A few months ago, she'd gotten involved with a rogue group of dissidents called the Blackcoats who'd sought to overthrow the Farthers with sabotage and vandalism, and she'd allowed my sister to join the group's dangerous activities against my wishes. The Blackcoats had tried to steal the Portable Locomotion Device from me, and Everiss had been with them. When she'd been shot in a confrontation with Korr, she'd come to us for shelter and brought the PLD as a peace offering. But I didn't trust her, even if she was technically on our side now.

She searched my eyes. "You didn't find anything."

"We found Adam Brewer's arrest warrant. He's in a prison in Astralux."

Everiss frowned. She barely knew Adam. He wasn't the one she was concerned about. She was worried about Ann Mayor, her—and my—best friend.

"What about Ann?"

I shook my head. Defeat tasted bitter on my lips as I spoke the words. "Nothing. I looked everywhere."

Everiss conveyed her disappointment only with a jerk of her chin. "Well, then. Jonn will want to know you're back safely."

I moved past her and into the room that now was our main living space. The ceiling arched up like a cave, disappearing into the darkness above. Shelves lined the walls, and the formerly dusty places had been filled with animal pelts and bundles of firewood. This had once been a debris-filled shell of some ancient library or archive room, but now it had become our communal quarters. We had precious little to ensure privacy, but everyone liked being close together because there was safety in numbers, and so far the Watchers had not bothered us behind these doors as long as we kept the halls filled with dried snow blossoms and the walls painted with depictions of the blue flowers.

People slept on pallets behind hanging sheets or spoke quietly to one another around the piles of glowing fungi that lit the space enough for us to see. It was early morning now, and most were sleeping, but some had already risen to begin cooking breakfast. My gaze wandered over the faces—they were haggard, worn from worry and exhaustion and lack of food. These were the fugitives who had returned with us from the past where they'd been living in hiding. I'd brought many of them back with me, many more than Atticus had wanted, and he had almost killed me for my failure. Jacob had intervened, and they'd both been slain by a Watcher. I hadn't forgotten Jacob's loyalty to me. I would repay him by caring for the fugitives now that he was gone.

I spotted my twin brother sitting at a table at the end of the room, and I headed toward him. He lifted his head and smiled at the sight of me, but his pleased expression faded when I reached him.

"What went wrong?" he asked.

I dropped into one of the chairs. It wobbled beneath my weight; the legs were uneven. "We found an arrest report for Adam, but nothing for Ann." I pulled the paper from the bag at my belt and set it on the table between us.

Jonn reached for it with one hand, smoothing away the crinkles. His forehead pinched as he scanned the information I'd already absorbed out in the forest.

"According to this paper," I said, "he was sent to a detainment facility in Astralux."

Astralux was the capital city of Aeralis, the Farther nation. I had never been there, but I'd heard stories about the dark, dank fog that constantly encompassed the city and swathed everything in moist gray, about the soldiers who paced the streets looking for dissidents, about the harsh laws and harsher people with their steam-powered machines and airships and guns. In my head I saw a place of smoke, cogs, and cruelty. And Adam was there—a prisoner, helpless, hopeless. I'd been holding out for information saying he was at a camp just beyond the Frost border, perhaps. Something that we actually might have been able to access, something we could reach. Astralux? He might as well be on the moon.

Jonn reached across the paper to grab my hand. He squeezed my fingers, and the pressure dragged me back to reality. I raised my eyes to his.

"We'll find out exactly where he is, Lia. We'll rescue him."

"I just..." I stopped. I didn't know what I wanted to say, so I clamped my lips shut and shook my head. Instead of finishing my thought, I rose and stalked across the room.

The fugitives who were awake fell silent as I passed. The ones who made eye contact with me offered tentative smiles, but nobody spoke to me. I was learning their names slowly, but I had been busy since our return, and I wasn't exactly in the most sociable mood. Honestly, I had far too much to worry about to waste any time on making small talk with them.

I spotted Juniper, the burly, bearded fugitive who'd found me when I passed through the gate. He sat beside a fire, stirring a pot of what looked like squirrel stew. The unappetizing smell of grease and burned meat wafted my direction, but I was hungry enough that my stomach rumbled anyway. Lately, we'd been eating anything we could get our hands on. We'd brought some supplies of canned goods and dried meats with us when we made the jump back to the Frost, but those things hadn't lasted us more than a week. Now, we relied on whatever we could trap or gather—or whatever my sister, Ivy, could bring us from the bag of food supplies she received each week in exchange for attending the Farther school in the village.

Juniper glanced up as I approached.

"Mothkat," he said, gesturing at the pot with a snort as he caught a glimpse of my expression.

I raised both eyebrows and bit back a sound of disgust. "Mothkat?" The scavengers—they essentially amounted to winged, vicious rats—were pests that preyed on dead animals and infested caverns and tree stumps. They had sharp teeth and were dangerous in large packs if provoked, but mostly they eschewed the living in favor of things that were already rotting. "Is it safe to eat that?"

"It's this or nothing," he said.

I didn't respond.

"How did your mission go?" he asked after a moment of silence. He stirred the bubbling pot and didn't look at me.

"It was not as successful as I'd hoped. We found no mention of one of my friends."

"Ann Mayor is her name?" he asked.

"Yes."

"If she was suspected of the same things as your other friend, why are they not imprisoned together?"

A fair question. "I don't know. I heard only that she was suspected of involvement, and that she had been sent to Astralux. But it is a massive city. I have no idea where to find her in it."

"Surely her father knows?" Juniper asked.

I sighed. "He knows nothing. No one does, except that Farther noble, Korr, and he's gone."

Juniper grunted in disappointment that his idea was not helpful.

Fatigue pulled at my eyelids and made my bones ache, but I couldn't sleep until I'd seen my sister. Ivy, who was almost fifteen and the youngest in my family, lived among the enemy now. She attended the Farther school by day and lived with the family of Bakers she'd been reassigned to, helping with their quota in the evenings. She learned whatever she could and stole away to meet with us at least once a week, and we expected her this morning. As a Weaver, her blood kept her safe in the forest just like mine kept me safe, and so I did not object to her making the long trek through the woods in the early hours of the morning for fear of Watchers. Still, I worried every time I knew she was coming, because there were many other dangers besides Watchers. Snow panthers, mothkats, bears, or even a Hunter or Trapper might run across her.

I returned to Jonn's side. He and Everiss were engaged in a conversation, and the sound of their voices reached my ears like the murmur of a stream. I stopped a few feet away, giving them privacy, but when they noticed me, she straightened and stepped away.

"Shouldn't you be sleeping?" Jonn asked in his scolding-but-affectionate way. "You've been up almost all night. You're going to get sick if you keep pushing yourself this way."

"Shouldn't you?" I countered. "You're the one who gets seizures."

"I can sleep whenever I want, since I never leave this room. You, on the other hand, are always chasing all over the Frost. You need rest."

He'd become more verbal lately, more assertive and direct. Throughout our childhood he'd always been the quiet one, content to follow my lead without arguing, the silent source of support who'd given me strength after our parents' deaths. He'd never done much beyond helping with the family quota and composing riddles and music for the amusement of Ivy and me, because his withered leg and frequent seizures had rendered him ineligible to take his full place as a grown man in the village, with all the privileges and responsibilities that such a role entailed. But now he gave orders and directed projects and bossed me about my sleeping habits.

My gaze slid to Everiss's bobbing hair as she sashayed across the room to speak with Juniper over the stewpot, and I wondered if the source of Jonn's sizzle had anything to do with the smile currently stretched across her face.

But my brother was waiting for my excuse, and I didn't feel like pondering the complicated relationship between him and Everiss Dyer. Not today. I sat, leaning both elbows on the table as I massaged my temples with my fingertips. "I'm expecting Ivy to show up this morning. I'm not going to miss her visit because I'm asleep."

"I'll wake you," he said, but then his eyes lit up, and I turned and saw a skinny, freckled girl with nut-brown hair and eyes too big for her face slip through the doors.

27

My sister. She clutched a bag in her hands. She always brought supplies—food and salt and soap, and sometimes a little sugar. She was like an angel, dispensing mercy in small doses just when we needed it most.

Ivy crossed the room at a brisk walk. My attention sharpened as I noticed she was limping.

"What happened to your leg?" I demanded.

She slid into the chair across from us. "Good morning, sister. I'm doing well, how are you?"

I shook my head. "I'm worried about that limp, that's what."

Jonn put his hand on my arm to silence me. "Glad to see you made it safely."

"The limp is nothing. I tripped and banged my ankle on a rock." She waved a hand dismissively and then reached into her sack. "Look, I brought sugar this time. A shipment came in from Aeralis."

My mouth watered in spite of everything, because sugar was a rare delicacy these days. A memory floated through my head—our mother, baking cookies with the precious ingredient, and Jonn and I sitting by the hearth weaving frantically because we couldn't have any until our quota was done for the day.

"How are things in the village?" Jonn asked.

"Not good," my sister muttered, running a finger across the table. "Raine has made another curfew, a tighter one. Quota has gone up because he's increased the number of soldiers in the village, but we have no way to realistically meet his demands and continue to feed ourselves properly. There is not enough food and not enough time. People are growing angry, desperate. Some are stealing from the soldiers' rations or trying to fudge their quota totals, but if they're caught, they are flogged, made to eat mud, left in stocks overnight until they get frostbite on their fingers. Raine always manages to be creative."

I grimaced. "And how are you managing?"

"I'm all right." Ivy glanced around the room and dropped her voice to a whisper. "How did the mission go?"

"Not as well as we had hoped."

"They found papers with Adam's location, but not Ann's," Jonn explained.

"And?" Ivy asked.

"It's far." I said the words softly, and the momentary despair that consumed me must have leaked into my voice, because my sister's face crumpled. She cared about Adam and Ann, too. They had been constants in her life as much as mine.

"Farther than you traveled to find me?" Gabe asked, grabbed a chair and sinking into it beside me.

Ivy didn't smile at Gabe, but the harsh planes of her face eased at his presence. He reached across the table and touched her hand in greeting.

"That's different," I said. "I used the gate."

"Can't you use the gate to travel to Astralux?"

Jonn shook his head. "We have to have a connecting portal, and the one in Echlos is the only one left as far as we know. It can connect to itself in the past, which is how we sent you and the others back, but we can't simply leap through it and expect to appear in another location in this time."

"What about the PLD? Isn't that a portal?"

"The PLD is here with us," I said. "So that wouldn't work, either. We'd have to go the old-fashioned way. On foot."

"There are trains past the border that run to Astralux," he said. "They run through the ice fields between the Frost and Aeralis, carrying wood and coal."

29

I visualized it—the black lines of the train tracks biting into the snow, the guards in their long coats, the harsh white and blue of the earth and sky. Gabe's breath, a cloud slipping from his lips. Mine matching. Running, our fingers slipping on cold metal as we tried to grab hold and hang on.

"We'll discuss it more later," Jonn said, and his voice pulled me back to the present. "Right now, you both need to sleep."

"We need to get in touch with the Trio," I said. "With Atticus dead and Adam missing, we have no leader."

"The Trio?" My sister's face wrinkled in confusion.

"They are the ones in charge of the Thorns. Their identities are secret, so I don't know their names...but I know Adam sent and received messages from them, so he must have had some way to contact them. I need to find out how. I need to tell them our situation here—the fugitives, Atticus's death—and I need to get our instructions. Maybe they can help us, send supplies, another leader."

"You are our leader now," Ivy said.

I snorted. "I've not been given that authority. And furthermore, I don't want it."

"You think they'd send someone else?" Gabe asked.

Jonn leaned across the table and rapped his knuckles in front of me. "You should sleep," he repeated. "Both of you."

"I want to know what happened to Ivy's leg first."

"No," she insisted. "I just tripped over a log."

"I thought you said you banged it on a rock."

She sighed loudly. "First I tripped over the log, then I hit it on the rock."

"Lia," Jonn said. "I really think you should let this go for now and get some rest."

This time, I acquiesced to him, because he was right. I needed rest. I was done arguing for the night.

Gabe helped me up, and his hand lingered a little on mine. I wondered if he was remembering our kiss earlier. Together we walked toward the cots that we'd pushed close together to make a makeshift place for the four of us—Jonn, Everiss, Gabe, and me.

"I'm truly sorry that we didn't find anything," he said once we'd reached the cots. "I know you miss him. I know you want him here again, safe. I don't..." he stopped.

Something knotted in my chest. This was a conversation that had been brewing between us for some time, but I was too tired to have it now. I started to shake my head, and Gabe put a finger to my lips.

"This isn't about me. You care about Adam...and I care about you. So we'll find him. Besides," he added with a twitch of a smile, "he saved my life. I should try to even the score." His eyes flicked to mine. "Sleep. You're not much of a talker when you're tired, Lia Weaver. Or any time, for that matter. I know better than to push my luck with you now."

I sank onto the nearest cot and tugged the blankets over my body. And before sleep claimed me, thoughts swirled in my head like birds before a storm. I found no rest from them.

THREE

THE SNOW CRUNCHED beneath my boots as I slipped through the Frost alone. All around me, the silence was broken by the crackle of snow falling and the musical sound of melting ice. Daylight sparkled on dripping icicles and glittered on the edges of wet pine needles.

The Thaw was coming, stronger every day, and the cold was damp, slipping inside my lungs and clinging to my clothes. My breath curled from my lips in a white vapor. My thoughts spiraled.

Earlier that day, I'd been to see Abel Brewer.

He didn't know anything about his brother's whereabouts. He'd moved methodically as we spoke, never stopping as he split logs and shoveled snow. He had barely looked at me. His face, haggard and etched with fatigue, was a study in neutrality. But his hands spoke another story. They were restless, harsh as they swung the axe and stripped bark from the wood. He didn't know how Adam had communicated with the Thorns leaders, he'd said. His brother spent much time wandering the Frost alone, he said. There were places that Adam used to go, he said. Places no one else knew about.

Places.

Now I was looking for such places.

Could these places contain some way to contact the Trio? Adam had kept contact with them somehow. I'd already searched the location where I'd once met Adam, a place not too far from my family's farm. But the hole in the ground contained little of value in regards to my quest, and I'd moved on. Now I roamed the Frost, seeking for any place where Adam might have kept the means to contact the Trio.

The wind caught the edges of my cloak and made it flutter as I squeezed between two tree trunks bent at awkward angles. Watchers had done it, maybe, although I didn't see any tracks. I scrambled over a rock and stopped to catch my breath.

As I did, I looked around me. The landscape was familiar, but in a faint, dreamy way. The trees were different, the rocks more exposed, and everything was blanketed in snow and ice.

I looked closer. There, at the edge of the trees, an almost imperceptible swell caught my eye. A roof, gently rounded beneath a bank of snow.

My lips curved in a smile. I knew this place. I'd seen it 500 years ago, in the distance past, before the Frost was cold. Before Watchers openly roamed. Before the Ancient Ones' society crumbled. This was the ruins of the private lab of Doctor Meridus Borde, my ancestor, the ancestor of all the Weavers with their special blood.

I approached the structure slowly. Centuries of forest decay covered the building. Only a small portion of the original dwelling still peeked above the surface. A tangle of brush obscured the place where the door had been.

I pushed the branches aside and stopped in astonishment. A path had been cleared through them, a recent path. It looked to be less than a year old, judging by the accumulation of debris and vegetation that had

33

gathered in the wake of the severed limbs and shoveled earth.

Was this Adam's doing?

My heart began to pound, and my fingers trembled as I pushed aside a few creeping tendrils of frost vine and stepped to the threshold. The door gave easily when I pushed against it, and I stumbled inside amid a shower of damp dirt and chunks of snow.

The wooden floor clattered under my feet. The air smelled faintly of dust and dried things. Sunlight streamed around me, illuminating the space.

The room vaguely resembled the place I remembered. Shelves cluttered with books and papers lined the walls. Two chairs lay on their sides, knocked over at some point and never righted again. Some of the legs were broken. Tables were crammed into every corner, piled high with strange inventions. I ran my fingers across a dust-covered cog and touched an opaque bubble of dark glass. What were these things? They looked like parts of some long-deceased monster of steel and brass.

I moved on toward the shelves. Glass crunched under my boots, and a draft of dusty air filled my nose. Memories assaulted me—memories of Borde showing me the journal he'd found, one that contained references to my family's riddles and to the Thorns. Where was that journal now? I searched the room but found nothing of value beyond a few books that I set aside to give to Jonn. Almost everything had crumbled into garbage. I looked for *The Snow Parables*, which I'd seen on these shelves 500 years earlier. My parents had owned such a book.

I didn't see it.

A chill skittered down my spine. Were the book I'd seen in the past and the book my parents possessed one and the same? How would they have gotten it?

Leaving the main room, I found the hall, a chasm of dusty darkness that echoed as I fumbled down it. I stumbled into what had been Borde's bedroom. A sagging mattress and disheveled sheets were barely visible from the light shining through the door in the main room. Where was the closet? Borde had kept a light-making device there. Ah, there was the door. I opened it.

My fingers bumped against metal as I groped in the darkness at the back of the closet shelves. I wrapped them around whatever I'd found and tugged, dragging out a long, narrow box.

The box was shiny, pristine, unlike the things in the main room that had deteriorated with time or neglect. I lifted it with a grunt and carried it to where the light was better. I jiggled the latch, but the box didn't open. I lifted it and shook, and I heard things sliding around.

There was something inside.

My investigations turned up nothing else. Finally, I picked up the box and pulled the door of the laboratory shut behind me. I would look again tomorrow for Adam's means of communication with the Trio. Cold air bit my cheeks as I plunged into the wilderness again, heading for home.

Before I'd gone too far, the snap of branches made me freeze. My muscles quivered as I held still and silent, listening. It couldn't be a Watcher—they didn't wander during the day—but there were any other number of lethal things roaming the Frost that might cross my path. Drawing my cloak around me, I eased back into a bush of snow blossoms and crouched close to the snow.

Something dark and alien moved clumsily through the white ten yards away. I filled my lungs with cold air and held the breath inside me.

Farther soldiers.

They moved furtively, their guns at ready and their eyes wide. Three of them, all thin and black like spiders against the blankness of the snow. They passed without seeing me and vanished around the bend, leaving only their footprints behind. They hadn't noticed mine, because I'd kept to the shady places beneath the trees where the snow didn't fall.

My heart beat staccato against my ribs, and my hands tingled. What were Farther soldiers doing here? Looking for me? For other Thorns agents? Or looking for something else entirely?

Maybe I could find out what it was.

I changed direction and doubled back, following the footprints they'd left behind in the snow. The murmur of their voices drifted on the wind, reaching my ears in an unintelligible garble. I needed to get closer if I wanted to hear what they were saying.

My feet whispered over the ground as I crept through the trees. Ice dripped down my neck and dampened the hem of my cloak. I pressed my back against a tree, and the bark scratched me through my clothes.

Ahead, the soldiers had stopped. They seemed to be arguing. One leaned against a tree, his arms folded. The other two stood a short distance away, studying the tracks of a Watcher. As I watched, one of the men picked ice off the bottom of his boot with a stick.

I listened.

"...Fool's errand anyway. Why Korr thinks we'll find that fugitive after all these months..."

They were looking for Gabe.

A month ago, I'd taken a gamble and given Korr information in order to gain access to his rooms and find the key that we needed to decode my da's old journals. I had told him that I'd seen Gabe in the Frost. That tidbit of knowledge must have been enough to motivate him to keep looking after he'd given up for months. And now he had his soldiers tramping around, poking through the snow, searching...what if they found footprints? What if they caught a glimpse of me, or one of the others?

I needed to warn Ivy, and anyone else who regularly made a trek through the Frost, lest they accidentally stumble across the enemy.

The soldiers moved on, and this time I let them go. I counted to fifty slowly in my head, and when all was silent once more, I headed back toward Echlos.

~

I reached Echlos with the box in tow and descended the staircases to the lowest level where we'd made our home. As the corridors echoed with my footsteps, someone stirred from a shadowy corner. I paused, apprehensive, until I recognized the face. It was Jullia, Everiss's sister. Like Ivy, she occasionally made the trek out to visit us and bring news and food, but she never came alone. My sister must be here, too.

"Lia," she said, relief filling her voice as she realized it was me. "I'd forgotten the way down...I'm glad you showed up." She stepped into the light, and her long gray cloak fluttered like a moth's wing.

"Where's Ivy?"

Jullia bit her lip. "She had something to do in the forest, she said. She told me to go on alone, and that she'd catch up."

"I saw Farther soldiers in the Frost not half an hour ago. Did you know they were making daylight expeditions this far?"

Jullia's eyes widened. "Soldiers? Outside the Cages? Raine has said nothing about it to the townsfolk. Are they...?" She dropped her voice. "Are they looking for you?"

I shook my head. She didn't know much about Gabe, really, and I wasn't going to volunteer that information. "They're looking for fugitives."

We reached the main rooms. Arla sat cross-legged before a small fire, cooking whatever disgusting gruel we were going to choke down for dinner. Juniper was by the cots, telling stories to entertain the two youngest fugitives, a girl and boy who rarely spoke. My heart softened a little as I looked at them, but I didn't stop. I went straight to Jonn's table and set the box on top of our da's miscellaneous papers that he was forever sifting through, looking for the answers to all his questions.

"Lia," he said in annoyance. "Don't put that here." He tugged one of the sheets of paper out from under it.

"I found it in the ruins of Borde's lab," I said.

Jonn paused at the mention of Borde. After a quick glance in my direction to confirm that I wasn't joking, he set down the paper and turned his full attention to the box. "What's inside?"

"Not sure. I couldn't get it open. But whatever it is, it seems to still be in good condition."

He fiddled with the latch, but it wouldn't give. "Hmmm."

Gabe joined us and leaned over the table with interest. "What's that?"

"I found it in Borde's old laboratory. We can't seem to get it open."

"Break it open?" he suggested.

I shook my head. "Not a good idea."

"What's inside might be fragile," Jonn murmured. He ran his fingers down the sides and over the lid. After a few moments of probing, he sat back and sighed.

"Whatever it is, someone has taken a great deal of care to make sure it's protected."

Everiss and Jullia joined us, their arms linked. I looked around to see if Ivy had arrived yet, but I didn't spot her among the cooking fires, or near the cot-tents, or at the little walled-off area of shelves where we'd gathered all the various old books and papers from the room for the fugitives to amuse themselves with when they became too bored.

"Where's Ivy?" Jonn asked.

"I don't know," Jullia said, her voice whisper-soft as she detected the note of concern in his voice. "She said it was nothing, a side trip."

Nothing could mean all sorts of things when it came to Ivy—a winterberry bush, a bird with a broken wing, a wounded fawn. My chest tightened with concern, though, because the Farther soldiers were in the forest, and my sister did not know. She was out blithely jaunting through the snow on some fool's errand when she could be in danger.

"I'll go find her," I said.

~

The land surrounding Echlos was mostly fields strewn with rocks. Icy mountains glittered in the north, silent sentinels separated from us by a black river and miles of craggy hills. To the south, forest concealed any dangers that might be lurking.

I slogged through the snow, which had half-melted in the sun and frozen again, making it look smooth and slick like glass instead of powdery white. I didn't dare shout Ivy's name because I had no idea how close or far those soldiers might be. I was confident they wouldn't come close enough to discover the Echlos buildings past the shimmer-shield that hid it from view, but if they heard voices, they might be compelled to examine the landscape a little closer. So I stayed quiet, listening to the sound of the bluewings shrieking in the trees.

Most of Echlos was buried deep underground, and the land around it, which had once been a series of gardens, had been reclaimed by forests and fields. Trees sprouted up between cracks in the roof and split crumbling walls in half. I slipped over a fallen limb and rounded the corner of the main laboratory building. A branch snapped beneath my heel, and the sound was loud in the silence.

I paused. The birds had been making so much racket a moment ago...why were they quiet now? I wrapped my cloak around me and crouched down. I held absolutely still. Was it the soldiers?

Faintly, I heard the sound of someone speaking quietly.

Ivy's voice.

Relief bubbled in my chest. I rose and turned the corner, ready to scold her for frightening us all. Ready to forgive her for whatever wounded animal she'd rescued this time. Ready to—

My legs locked and my lungs deflated as I saw what loomed in front of me. In front of Ivy.

A Watcher.

FOUR

"IVY, A WATCHER!" I shouted.

"Lia?" Ivy whirled, her eyes wide and her hands fluttering out to stop me. "What are you doing here?"

"Don't just stand there! Cut your finger!"

She didn't move.

Panting, I yanked my knife from my belt and pressed the point to my finger. A droplet of blood beaded against the tip of the blade, scarlet on steel.

The Watcher snarled and pawed the ground. It was big, twice the size of a horse. Eyes that burned amber swiveled to regard me. I didn't have time to wonder why a Watcher was out here in the daylight, why it hadn't killed us yet, or why Ivy was here in the first place. I drew the knife across my finger and felt the blood rush out as sweet as relief. It splattered against the snow below. The Watcher jerked away, its limbs shuddering.

"Stop!" Ivy shook her head, her long hair flying everywhere. "Stop it. He won't hurt us. He isn't dangerous."

I barely heard her. Still brandishing the knife in my bleeding hand, I dragged her with me around the side of the building and out of the beast's line of sight. Ivy tried to shake me off.

"Come on," I said. "There are Farther soldiers in the woods, and that Watcher is out there in *broad daylight*, and we've got to get inside before anything else goes wrong."

Ivy's face paled. "Farther soldiers?"

"Yes. Come on."

She stopped fighting me, and we ran for the entrance to the ruins, not slowing until the shade of the first tunnel covered our faces. As soon as we were inside, I turned and slammed her against the wall.

"What is going on?"

She gulped air. Her hands grabbed my wrists, but she didn't struggle. "I don't know why Farther soldiers would be in the—"

"That's not what I mean. What were you doing out there? With a *Watcher?*" I remembered a flash of what I'd seen—she'd faced it defenseless, unafraid. She hadn't been cowering or fleeing. She hadn't screamed for help. She'd been *talking* to it. And she'd fought me when I tried to intervene. "What's going on?" I repeated.

A vein in her throat pulsed. She licked her lips. "It's not what you think."

"What, you mean this isn't some wounded baby raccoon that you can bring home? That's right, Ivy. It's a Watcher. I saw one break two men's necks a few weeks ago as easily as I might break a twig." I snapped my fingers, and she flinched.

"I..."

"Tell me," I demanded.

She shut her eyes and turned her face away from me. "He isn't dangerous," she murmured.

I barked a laugh at the sheer absurdity of that statement. My sister, ever the insane one. Farther fugitives, Blackcoats, and now this? Trying to cozy up to a Watcher? She'd finally embarked on her greatest mission of misguided mercy yet. "How long have you had this delusion?"

42

"I've been visiting him for almost two months," she mumbled.

"Two months," I repeated, thunderstruck. And it hit me—all the times when she'd been out in the woods claiming to be gathering berries. Had she been doing this instead? And what exactly was...this?

"Tell me everything." My tone left no room for argument, and she made none. With a shaking voice, she recounted a wild tale of stumbling across a "wounded" Watcher in the forest, and how she'd taken pity on it and eventually befriended it. Or rather, him, as she kept saying. As if a Watcher could be male or female.

"They are machines, Ivy. They aren't alive. They can't feel."

"I know they're machines," she countered. "I've seen where they sleep. They need sunlight for strength. It's why they only come out at night."

I've seen where they sleep... She knew where the Watchers' lair was? Where they went during the day?

"That one was out in daylight," I countered.

"They can come out during the day if they're activated. They're more docile then, less prone to attacking. But that one is especially safe. He's friendly."

"No Watcher is safe," I said. "I don't want you going near one ever again."

"Lia—"

But there wasn't time to argue about it now. We needed to get below before anyone else came looking for us. But the conversation was far from over. "We'll talk about this more later, Ivy Weaver," I said, and dragged her with me down the corridor.

We reached the room where the others waited. Jonn and Gabe were both sitting at the table, and I stalked toward them.

"Don't tell them," Ivy begged, grabbing my sleeve.

43

I had no intention of keeping her secret. I shook my head and continued walking, and when I reached the table I opened my mouth to spill everything. But Jonn spoke first.

"The Blackcoats have sent us a message."

The Blackcoats. The band of vigilantes who'd formed to deal with the "Farther problem." So far, they'd managed to get several of their members killed, arrested, or injured. And they'd only succeeded in making Raine angry, like hornets stinging a bull. Apprehension filled me.

"How did they find out where we are?" I demanded. "Who delivered this message?"

Jonn looked at Jullia.

"I received this to pass along to the Thorns," she said softly, withdrawing a folded piece of paper and handing it to me.

"Who knows that you have contact with us?"

She simply shook her head.

I unfurled the note. My fingers were still shaky from the encounter with the Watcher.

To Whom It May Concern,

Previously our two groups have had divergent goals, but the time has come to band together against a greater enemy. The Farthers will consume us all if we do nothing. If you are willing to consider ways that we might work together, meet us at the Hunters' clearing beside the river at midnight in three days' time.

—the People for the Freedom of the Frost

"The People for the Freedom of the Frost?" I asked.

"That's what they call themselves now," Ivy said, the first words she'd spoken since we'd returned. "They have new leaders, new objectives. It is not just young people now. Many villagers have joined, more and more as Raine's policies and excesses become more intolerable."

"What else has changed?" I was too agitated to sit, so I paced.

"Raine confiscates property or arrests those he considers suspicious on trumped-up charges," she explained. "The soldiers are everywhere. Food is scarce. Everyone is angry and restless. If we strike now—"

"We?"

She was silent.

I couldn't speak. Had she rejoined the Blackcoats in addition to her insanity with the Watchers? I wanted to shake her. But I only curled my fingers into fists and turned to the others. When I spoke, my voice was sharp as a knife's blade.

"How exactly did you come by this message?" I shot a look at Jullia, who withered beneath it.

"It appeared in my bag," she whispered. "No one spoke to me. They do not know where you are, or even that you are alive, Lia. The whole village thinks that you and your brother have either fled or perished. Ivy has been reassigned a home. She is in essence an orphan now. And no one questions that, although I think there are some who suspect Everiss still lives in hiding and has joined the Thorns, hence their using me as a contact."

"Do they think we'll trust them?" Anger threatened to choke me. The Blackcoats had put my sister in danger. They'd tried to steal the PLD for their own purposes. They'd behaved foolishly and recklessly. Everiss had almost died because of their mishandling of things. And

45

now they wanted to join with us and muck up our plans? "What could they possibly want from us?"

"The Blackcoats think that we could expel the Farthers for good if we joined forces," Jonn said. He rubbed a finger against his chin. "And they might be right."

My blood turned to steam.

"This," I said, "is one of the stupidest things I've ever heard you say, Jonn Weaver."

He turned his head to looked at me. "Oh?"

"Yes!" I threw up my hands. "I can't believe...are you truly going to make me formulate a protest against this insanity?"

"You're not even listening," Ivy protested. "You're saying no without thinking this through."

"Ivy makes a good point," Jonn said.

"Ivy has been making lots of bad decisions lately," I snapped. "Right now her judgment is seriously in question. And I don't have to 'think this through.' The Blackcoats are foolish and incompetent, as they've demonstrated previously by getting their own leader shot and many of their members injured or arrested. Collaboration with them will most likely reveal our identities and get us killed. Right now we need to lie low, marshal our resources, contact the Trio, and find our friends."

Everiss sat beside Jonn, her lips pressed in a straight line and her arms crossed. I couldn't tell what she thought about this. She claimed she had no ties to them any longer, but I wasn't so sure of her loyalties. Jonn reach out and touch her elbow lightly, and she shot him a glance. The wordless exchange contained a library of information, but I didn't have time to ponder it now.

"We're not doing this," I said. "I refuse."

Jonn opened his mouth to reply, but another voice beat him to it.

"Well, you aren't the only one who makes the decisions around here."

I swung around in surprise to see Gabe standing behind us. His cheeks were flushed with anger, and his body was stiff.

"Gabe," I said, taking note of his posture, his expression. He was angry.

"How long were you planning on discussing this before you told me what was going on?"

"You're not..." I began to say, and stopped. Something inside me turned brittle, and it felt like regret. I shouldn't have gone down that path, not here. Not now.

"Not a member of the village? Not a true inhabitant of the Frost?" Gabe asked, speaking solely to me. "You think I don't have a stake in what happens here? Is it because I'm a Farther, too?"

Words rose in my throat and stuck there.

"I just don't trust them," I said finally.

"They have a new leader now." Jonn spoke as if I were a horse that had gotten spooked in its stall and needed calming. I bristled at that tone—I didn't need soothing—but I listened. I'd spoken my piece, now I might as well let him speak his.

"Those who haven't been arrested are the clever ones," he argued. "The ones who learn from their mistakes. And they have many new members."

"Things have gotten bad in Iceless," Jullia said softly. "Raine is threatening everyone. Food is scarce. Some have lost their homes. Many more have been punished—put in stocks, flogged, just like I told you before. The villagers all want to do something, but they're afraid."

47

They all watched me, their gazes sharp as they waited for my response, and suddenly my arms and legs seemed heavy as rocks. Exhaustion burned behind my eyes.

"I'm going for a walk."

I turned and headed for the corridors, my cloak whispering around my ankles.

~

I wandered through the halls of Echlos, pacing past ruined labs and through crumbling doorways until I reached the place I sought—the echoing chamber that held the gate. The massive round eye slumbered in silence while beams of sunlight lanced the air around it and turned dust motes gold and glittery. Memories haunted this room now—memories of Gabe leaving me, of Atticus urging me forward into the unknown to find him again, of us returning with far more fugitives than anyone had planned for. Now I shouldered a great burden, one I hadn't asked for, hadn't wished for. What did they want from me? Did they want me to keep them alive, or did they want me to nod and say yes to whatever idiot schemes they dreamed up next?

I needed Adam and his advice. The profound hole left by his absence ached within me.

Footsteps crunched on the debris behind me. I turned.

Gabe leaned in the doorway, hands in his pockets, eyes on the gate. He chewed his lip, and I could see that he was sorting words in his head. His eyes were tired. The silence curled around me like ice and hardened, holding me prisoner.

"Do you remember how we felt that night?" he asked. "The night I went through that gate?"

I exhaled in a shaky laugh. "I remember well."

The silence tightened again, squeezing me. I had so many things that I wanted to say. But they were sharp things, and I was afraid.

"I miss him," I said finally. The admission made me feel naked.

His chest rose and fell in a breath. "I know. I can see it in everything you do."

The rest of the things I wanted to say seemed too fragile, as if the words would shatter as they left my lips. I laced my fingers together and turned back to the gate. Pain throbbed in my chest in time with my heartbeat. "I'm sorry about earlier," I said. "You aren't from the Frost, but it's your home now, too."

"It's hard to get used to." His admission of vulnerability was a gesture of forgiveness. I understood that. I stepped toward him, wanting to be near him.

"Do you miss Aeralis?" I asked.

"More than I know how to say." He moved closer, close enough that he could take my hand if he wanted, but he didn't. We stood side by side, gazing at the gate, a gate that could transport travelers across the world, but couldn't take either of us home. "My father's house—the palace—is built of black stone and surrounded by gates of wrought iron. It's an imposing place, I suppose, but I always loved it. Fog wraps the city in darkness most of the time, so our gardens were all enclosed in glass houses. I played in them for hours every day. The air was so damp and hot that my hair would curl and moisture would drip from my nose." He paused. "It is so dry here. So cold and dry."

I inhaled a lungful of sweet, icy air and let it out. Through the hole in the ceiling, a patch of blue sky glowed like a sapphire. The wind blew, scattering shards of ice that prickled our faces.

"Steam rises from pipes on the roofs of the houses and fills the air," he continued, wistful. "It's always misty there. The lights catch the fog and glow. The whole city glows, like a painting where all the colors run together. The whole city breathes the same breath. Here...here everything is stripped bare, stark, wild."

"Free," I said simply. He didn't disagree, but by the look on his face, the word meant different things to him.

I wanted to apologize for earlier, but that seemed too heavy amid this gossamer mood of memory. "What do you think of the note from the Blackcoats?" I asked instead.

He considered the question. His forehead wrinkled. "I think you are right to be wary, Lia. From what your brother and you have told me, the Blackcoats made a mess of things before. But," and he lifted both eyebrows as he said the word, "the Blacksmith's son is dead now. There is a new leader. Things might be different."

"Is it worth that risk?" I argued. "Right now we have two goals: rescue our friends and contact the Trio. The Blackcoats have nothing to do with that."

"If we can drive the soldiers from Iceless, we will no longer have to live in this ruin," Gabe said. "And everything will be easier."

That, if nothing else, was sensible. I hesitated. "I will think on it," I said.

He nodded, satisfied, and said nothing more. I might have reached for his hand in that moment, but before I could he lifted it to scratch his neck. We continued to stand together, inches apart but experiencing the same silence. Then I thought of Adam, and pain radiated from my chest.

I needed Adam here. He was my partner, my confidante, and I felt lost without him. But he was gone, and I had no choice but to go on alone.

"All right," I said. "We can meet with the Blackcoat leaders to discuss the possibility. But I don't trust them. And I don't like it."

FIVE

THE DARKNESS OF night enveloped me as I journeyed to meet the Blackcoat leaders three nights later. Every inch of me screamed to turn back, but I kept moving forward, slipping between tree trunks and ducking around ice-covered boulders that jutted from the forest floor like broken teeth in the mouth of a monster. I had to do this. Adam was gone. I was the one everyone was counting on, and the weight of that knowledge pressed against me like a pile of stones.

But I did not go completely alone. Gabe, Arla, and Everiss kept pace beside me, though we moved through the night without speaking. Everiss's curly hair bobbed in the places where it had escaped from her braid, the tendrils visible where the hood of her cloak had slipped back. Her eyes were huge in her face when she turned to look at me. It was her first time in the Frost since we'd fled my family's farm a few weeks ago, and in the moonlight I could see her hands shaking.

Gabe was silent and grim, as he always was in the Frost. He was frightened too, but he hid it better. Only I knew him well enough to read the way he moved and know it meant he was two breaths away from panic. But he pressed on anyway, never hesitating. Beside him, Arla did the same.

We all wore long, dark cloaks. Scarves covered our mouths and noses, and hoods drooped over our eyes, almost obscuring them. To an observer, I would be unrecognizable, as would Gabe and Everiss. It was exactly as we wanted it, because I was supposed to have fled the Frost, Everiss was supposed to be dead, and Gabe bore a striking resemblance to Korr. We all had our secrets to keep.

We reached the river that flowed black as ink alongside the road marking the end of the Frost and the beginning of Aeralis, the Farther world. We'd agreed to meet the new Blackcoat leaders here in the Hunters' clearing, a place where Hunters stored extra weapons and traps. The snow-filled circle lay undisturbed. Nothing stirred in the darkness.

I crouched in the bushes and pressed my back against the rough bark of one of the trees. Gabe and Arla took their places beside me, and Everiss crept forward alone. Her boots whispered across the scabby mixture of ice and mud that coated the ground. She reached the center of the clearing and stopped.

A branch snapped in the distance. I straightened, straining to see.

The darkness rippled, and three figures emerged.

Blackcoats?

Everiss stiffened but didn't move. She raised a hand in greeting, and the three figures halted. One stepped forward alone to meet her. It was too dark to distinguish faces, and they all wore plain black cloaks that hung over their eyes, much like ours did.

I signaled for Gabe and Arla to circle around behind them through the trees.

The figure who had come forward spoke. It was a man. His voice was muffled.

"Thank you for agreeing to meet us. Can we have some proof of who you are?"

53

Everiss nodded and produced the silver symbol of the Thorns, a broken Y-shaped branch with tiny pricks. "Do you recognize this?"

The man nodded. His shoulders relaxed.

Gabe and Arla rejoined me and shook their heads to show that no one was hiding in the woods behind the figures. Satisfied by now that the Blackcoats were alone, I rose from the bushes. The cloaked heads swiveled in my direction. I thought I saw one reach toward his waist, as if going for a weapon, but he relaxed when he realized I was with Everiss.

"You said you wanted to talk," I said, lowering my voice and making it sound gruff. "So talk."

The first figure spread his hands in a gesture of friendship and nonaggression . He wore gloves, black like the rest of his attire. "We need your help. Things have become dire in the village, as you may know. Officer Raine is driving our people to starvation. Children are being indoctrinated and their parents allow it so they can get a little more food. Honest citizens are having their property confiscated."

"You should speak with your Mayor," I said sharply. "He was the one who promised this would be temporary and beneficial to all."

The Blackcoat flinched. "The Mayor is powerless to act against Raine alone. That's why we need your help."

"Plan on blowing up any more buildings?"

He winced at the mention of their previous reputation. "That was the old way. We are choosing a different path."

"And what's in it for us?" I demanded. I couldn't let them know how afraid I was. I couldn't let them know anything but ruthlessness. They couldn't gain a foothold in this conversation. My voice was strong as steel, but beneath the folds of my cloak, my legs trembled.

"We can help you," he said. "We know you hide in the forest. We know the Frost would make an excellent point of connection for your other operations. We will partner with you. With the soldiers gone, you can move freely, and you won't have to live in the wilderness."

No more hiding and skulking and bedding down in ruins. I ached to think about it. My bones were cold and my blood half-frozen. And in my mind, a single image crystallized.

With the Farther soldiers gone—with Raine gone—I could have my family's farm back.

But was this the best decision for everyone? My own desires tugged at me selfishly, but I hesitated.

"You'll have to do better than that," I answered. "I need specifics, promises. We will need places for refugees from across the river to stay. Those of us who are Frost natives must have their property returned."

"It will be done," the man said.

I couldn't trust them. Not yet. "I'll have to speak with my superiors," I said. "We will contact you with our answer."

The Blackcoat nodded. He retreated into the forest, followed by his companions. Everiss and I rejoined Arla and Gabe, and we headed for Echlos.

~

Jonn gazed placidly at me across the table as I paced. He held a long, slender tool in his hand, and he was using it to try to open the box I'd found in the ruins of Borde's lab.

"I don't know if we should do this," I said for the tenth time.

"It's a smart move for us to make," he said, twisting his wrist gently to the left and lowering his ear to the lock. "They're right, you know. We can't keep living this way. We need a better location. The Farthers are starving the town, and we are hanging on by our fingernails out here. If we can work together to drive them away, we should."

I faced him and took a deep breath. "I want the farm back, Jonn."

His eyelashes flickered, and I knew he did, too. He straightened and set down the tool.

"We'll get it," he promised me.

I didn't share his hope.

~

I crouched at the edge of the wall of forest that separated the Frost from civilization. With shaking fingers, I moved a snow-covered branch and peered through the hole in the foliage that I'd made. Across a yard blanketed with snow, I saw it.

My family's farm.

Footprints crisscrossed the yard, trampling a muddy path from the front door to the barn. The paddock held three horses with shaggy coats and droopy heads. Faintly, I heard the sound of laughter drift on the wind.

Something hot and furious brewed in my stomach.

"What is this place?" Arla whispered from where she knelt beside me. "I thought we were supposed to be checking traps."

"It's my family's farm," I said. "My home."

"Oh." She breathed the word reverently, because the idea of home ignited a worshipful feeling in all of us these days. "I remember it now. I came here before the gate."

"Stay here." I shoved back the branches and stepped through the perimeter of trees into the yard. My heart pounded a sick rhythm against my ribs, making me dizzy, but I didn't stop until I'd reached the whitewashed walls of the farmhouse. I inched along the side until I reached a window. Moving so slowly that my muscles screamed in protest, I lifted my head and peered through the glass.

The curtains were only half-drawn, so I could see into the main room. The furniture was all in disarray— my ma's chair was shoved against the wall, and the other chairs drawn close to the fire. Pairs of muddy boots lay around the hearth, and someone's socks were strewn across the floor.

My throat squeezed.

As I watched, a man stepped into view. He rubbed a hand through his tangled hair and scratched beneath one arm. He wore an unbuttoned gray coat with brass buttons.

Farther soldiers were living in my family's farmhouse.

I shivered with rage. My pulse throbbed in my ears, and my hands were clenched so tightly into fists that my fingernails dug into my palms through my gloves. I dropped back into a crouch and crept back along the wall.

"What is it?" Arla asked when I reached her again. "Is something wrong?"

I shook my head, unable to articulate the storm building inside me. "Let's just keep going. We have to check the traps."

We pushed through the web of branches obscuring the path, moving gingerly around jutting rocks and fallen limbs. Flashes of blue filled my vision as we passed banks of snow blossoms growing wild. Their scent perfumed the air and tickled my nose. Beside me, Arla sneezed.

I paused. The birds had fallen silent. Was it our passage that frightened them, or something else? The skin on the back of my neck crawled.

Arla craned her neck to see around us. "Did you hear—?"

A gunshot rang out, and Arla cried aloud. "Lia!"

Soldiers.

I swung around, scanning the trees, but I saw nothing except the wet black of branches and the blinding white of snow. No flutters of gray. No glint of weapons.

"Lia," Arla said again.

"Run," I gritted out.

I grabbed her arm and pushed her forward, following behind her, scrambling into the cover of the trees and up a snow-crusted bank. It had to be a patrol like I'd seen before, the one looking for Gabe. We must have stumbled across one of their circuits by mistake. We had to double back, disguise our tracks, take the long way to Echlos. We couldn't lead them to the others.

"This way," I hissed. "We'll head west and circle back around."

Arla staggered, and I caught her with both hands. My palms came away slick with blood. Red bloomed across the side of her cloak.

"It hurts." Her eyes were wild as they met mine. Dread struck me to the bone, but I shoved it deep down where it couldn't paralyze me. I didn't have to time to do anything but act.

"Come on. We have to keep moving."

She nodded. Her skin was draining of color and her eyes were dulling. I took her by both shoulders and shook her. "Stay with me," I commanded. "Arla!"

"Keep moving," she repeated in a painful whisper.

I slipped one arm beneath her shoulder and wrapped it carefully around her wounded side. She sucked in a breath, the only sound she made as I touched the wound accidentally.

Together, we hobbled west, stopping frequently to duck into the bushes and wait for the sounds of pursuit. Every time we stopped, Arla sagged to the ground and wheezed as if unable to breathe. I bent over her, frantic as I scanned her expression. Had the bullet punctured a lung?

"You're going to be fine," I said again and again. "We'll get you back. The others will know what to do."

"Yes," she murmured. "I'll be fine, Lia. I crawled my way into the Frost with a broken leg before your parents found me."

I tried to help her up again, but she couldn't rise. Her eyes fluttered closed, and her breathing slacked.

"Arla," I whispered, frantic. "Arla!"

She didn't respond. Her lips began to turn gray, and her skin waxy. Her hand dropped from mine into the snow. I cradled her in my arms as a burning pressure built in my throat and behind my eyes.

She was dead.

I made a single, strangled sound as her body cooled against me and my thoughts spun with rage and grief and shock.

~

"She died bravely."

I stood before the shallow grave we'd dug. A mound of snow, covered with snow blossoms, made a stark hill in the middle of the white plain before Echlos' entrance.

Grief sat like a stone on my heart. She'd been in my care. And she'd died.

"She didn't give up. She kept going until she couldn't go any more..."

My words faltered. I drew in a shuddering breath. It was a pitiful eulogy. I was no good at speeches.

"She shouldn't be dead," I finished.

"It isn't your fault," Gabe said. He stood beside me, holding a shovel. A few of the other fugitives clustered around us, looking down at the grave. No one else spoke.

"No. Not mine. It's their fault. The soldiers. Raine. This whole occupation."

I ground my teeth together and turned back toward Echlos. I would give the Blackcoats their answer.

SIX

THE ROOFS OF the village gleamed silver in the moonlight, like a ragged mountain range topped with ice. I held my breath as I waited for the Farther soldier on the wall to pass, and then Gabe and I ran together to the place where we could squeeze through the wall and into the village. My lungs hurt and my whole body sparked with apprehension, but I shoved away every feeling and focused on the world around me—the dull rasp of my boots against the cobblestones, the hiss of my breath joining the wind that whipped around us, the thud of my knuckles knocking against the door below the sign of the Blacksmith.

Hinges creaked, a swath of light split the night, and then we were drawn inside a bright room by reaching hands. The door shut behind us, and light momentarily blinded my eyes.

I blinked as my vision adjusted. We stood in the back room of the blacksmith shop. Shuttered windows lined the walls, and a ladder led to an upstairs room in the far corner. Tables and benches were shoved back to make space to stand.

Four figures dressed in black shirts and trousers stood before us. I recognized them all, but only vaguely—one was a Fisher, and one was an older man who worked as a Tanner. The third, a woman, was the sister of Leon Blacksmith, the former Blackcoats leader who had been shot by Korr as he tried to steal the PLD from me. Unlike us, their faces were uncovered except for one final figure. Based on his height and the shape of his shoulders, I guessed he was the leader from last time we'd met. He wore a black scarf around his nose and mouth just as Gabe and I did, and I couldn't see his face. A pair of tired eyes peered at me over the cloth. He didn't blink.

"Show us the sign," Laina demanded. She was a brown-haired, slender woman with chapped hands and a freckled nose.

I pulled out the silver brooch that had belonged to my parents before me. The Blackcoats relaxed visibly.

"You aren't going to show your faces?" Laina asked.

"No," I said, speaking again in a low, gruff voice so they wouldn't recognize mine, even though I doubted they would. "We wish to keep our faces to ourselves." I nodded at their masked leader. "And him?"

"The same," the figure said, and his voice was equally muffled.

"This is Sam Fisher and Yoel Tanner, and I am Laina Blacksmith," she said, pointing to each in turn as she named them. "And your names?"

I hesitated. I had not prepared an alias.

"Garrett," Gabe said quickly, using the name he'd gone by in the past. They all nodded in greeting.

I followed his lead. "Lila," I said. "Lila...Bluewing."

A few eyes widened, and they smiled.

The bluewing, that tiny, plucky bird that dared to live within the poisonous embrace of the stingweed, had always been an inspiration to those who lived in the Frost. They recognized the reference, and clearly appreciated it.

The masked leader stepped forward. "Thank you for agreeing to meet. I know we all take a great risk in doing so. Raine grows increasingly suspicious every day. He is receiving pressure from Aeralis, although we don't know why or to what end. The nobleman Korr continues to ask questions, too. He's up to something and cannot be trusted."

Gabe and Laina both stiffened at the mention of Korr. Laina, I supposed, was thinking of her brother. And Gabe was thinking of his.

"And what do you want us to do?" I asked.

"We want to take back Iceliss," Laina said. Her eyes glittered as she spoke, and her fingers curled into fists. "And we need your people's help."

"But you live in the village," I pointed out. "We live outside it. Why do you need our help?"

Laina crossed her arms. "Your people are skilled in gathering information. You know the Frost, the forests. You are brave and strong and cunning. We need you if we want to have any hope of defeating the Farthers."

"Some of us—most of us—*are* Farthers," I said. "The old Blackcoats wanted nothing to do with Aeralians or sympathizers. Are you still willing to work with us, knowing who we are?"

The masked figure spoke. "The enemies of our enemies are our friends."

"My brother felt differently," Laina said. "He's dead now. I do not want to follow in his ways."

I looked at Gabe and he looked at me. All I could see was the glimmer of his eyes shining in the lamplight. He nodded slightly, giving his support, and I turned back to the Blackcoats. I reached out my gloved hand, and Laina took it.

"We—" I began.

A pounding sound filled the air, and a harsh voice called for someone to open the door. I froze. Laina's mouth fell open, and she jerked back as the oak panels behind us shuddered.

"Soldiers," she hissed.

A piece of the door splintered away. I saw a flash of hardened faces and gray uniforms, and a wave of dizziness shot through me along with a single, penetrating realization.

We were going to be caught.

Laina screamed for us to run. Gabe grabbed me by both shoulders and pushed me forward as Farther soldiers streamed inside the room.

We scattered. Laina and Sam fled for the back. Yoel threw open a window and wriggled out. The masked Blackcoat had already vanished.

"This way," I called to Gabe as I ran for the ladder that led to the second story. He was right behind me. The soldiers yelled for us to halt, but we climbed without stopping.

I reached the top and scrambled onto the wooden floor with Gabe right behind me. We ran for the window, and I threw it open. Beyond, shingles glimmered with ice, but we had no other choice. My fingers dug into the frame as I hoisted myself through the hole. My feet slipped, and Gabe grabbed my hands.

"Careful."

I felt around with my heels until I found purchase against the roof. Behind me, the shutters splintered, and Gabe tumbled out as something whistled past my ear. Bullets.

The soldiers were shooting at us.

"Come on." He pushed me forward, and we slid down the incline of the roof toward the ground. I slipped from the edge and landed in a bank of snow. Gabe's hands found mine again, and we ran.

We had to get out before the soldiers found us.

Wind whipped through my hair and snagged my cloak. I ran down a narrow alley and turned a tight corner with Gabe at my side. We were a few streets away from the break in the wall. Shouts and footsteps rang out behind us. I ran faster, turning another corner. Almost there—

Hands grabbed my cloak and yanked me into a dark room. I fought, kicking and clawing, and someone yelped and cursed. I was shoved against a wall.

"It's us, it's us, stop fighting!"

I recognized that voice. Laina. I paused, and the person holding me took the opportunity to pin my wrists firmly in place against the wall. Someone behind her lit a match, and it flared in the blackness with a hiss.

Laina released me, and I grabbed my scarf to make sure it was still in place. She peered at me, her shoulders rising and falling with her rapid breathing, her lashes coal-black against her white face. "Are you all right?"

I pushed away from the wall and looked for an exit. We were in another back room of another shop. Rows of barrels stood beneath the windows.

"You betrayed us," I spat. "The deal's off."

"We didn't! I don't know how they found us!"

Two other figures materialized from the darkness. Yoel Tanner and the Blackcoat with his face obscured. Laina turned. "Where's Sam?"

"They got him," Yoel said, his eyes shifting from hers to mine.

Laina covered her mouth with one hand. She blinked, shook her head, and her expression smoothed as she turned back to me.

"We have to speak quickly. You see now how it is here, what we must endure. Will you help us?"

"We can hardly believe you now," Gabe snarled from his place beside me. "Especially him." He gestured at the Blackcoat with the concealed face. "He could be anyone. He could be Raine himself."

"You'll just have to trust us—"

Trust. Ha. I headed for the door with Gabe following me.

"Wait," the unknown Blackcoat called.

We stopped.

"As a show of good faith..." He reached up to undo his scarf.

The other Blackcoats tensed. I held my breath. And as the fabric fell away, I leaned back hard against the wall.

Before me stood the Mayor of Iceliss.

SEVEN

JONN STARED AT me. "The Mayor is the new leader of the Blackcoats?"

"I saw it with my own eyes."

He ran both hands through his hair. "What does this mean?"

I sighed. "It means people are finally getting fed up with Raine, all the way to the top of the chain of command. And...I think it means we can really do this. With the Mayor on our side, we'll have access to everything."

"But can we trust him?" Gabe interjected. "He's not exactly the most reliable of people. He's the one who betrayed the village in the first place, isn't he?"

"I know," I said. "And you're right. Whatever reason he has for doing this, it's probably solely for his own benefit. But if there's one thing that's true about the Mayor, it's that he looks out for himself. We can count on that, at least."

"So what is the plan?" Jonn asked.

"We meet them again in a week to discuss it. For now, I need everyone working on ideas," I said. "Jonn, I'm putting you in charge of coordination of our part of the project. Everiss, you know the craftsmans' quarter of the village better than the rest of us. You can help Jonn draw up a map. Pay special attention to any back alleyways or unused buildings that we might be able to take advantage of. Gabe, you know the most about the Aeralian perspective. How they fight, how they strategize...what makes them tick."

Everyone nodded solemnly.

"What about me?"

I turned. Ivy stood in the doorway, her cloak wet with snow, a bundle of supplies dangling from her hand.

"You and I," I said, "need to talk."

She followed me out of the common room and into the hall, but I didn't stop there. I climbed the winding staircase until we were alone in one of the upper corridors of Echlos. The air around us smelled like dust and dirt, and I could hear the wind blowing far away.

Ivy crossed her arms and pressed her lips together. She knew what was coming.

"I've been busy with this Blackcoats business," I said. "But I haven't forgotten about you."

"It isn't—"

"Listen to me," I said. "You cannot fool around with the Watchers. They are not the same thing as a wounded bluewing or a baby rabbit. They are not even the same thing as a Farther fugitive. We've indulged you our entire lives, Ivy, but this is the end of the line. This is insanity."

"You don't understand." Tears had begun to seep from her eyes. "He won't hurt me."

"That's because you're a Weaver," I hissed. "Your blood keeps you safe from attack. They won't harm *us*. But you could get someone else killed. They are not safe. Don't ever let yourself be fooled into thinking they are."

"But they feel. They think. They learn..."

"Sophisticated," I said. "But not capable of caring about you. So stop fooling yourself."

She shook her head. "You just don't understand."

"Ivy..." My patience was beginning to fray. I stepped toward her, but she brushed my hand away and moved farther down the hall.

"I've been studying them," she said. "Learning more about them. We know next to nothing except what has been handed down in rumors and folklore. The more information we have, the more we can do with it. Don't you see? Besides...they are fascinating."

"It isn't safe." I had to work to keep myself from shouting. Why did I have to keep reminding her of this?

"For instance," she continued, ignoring me, "I've learned that they are not so dangerous in daylight. They're calmer. They don't attack automatically, and they don't roam aimlessly or hunt on their own. Like you saw yourself, they *can* move in daylight hours—but they have to be summoned. Otherwise, they shut down automatically. But if they are summoned, they move and explore and can be taught. They're...curious."

"Summoned?"

"Awakened, I guess."

"So you are voluntarily awakening Watchers in the day time? Do you understand how dangerous that is? How many lives you're putting at risk?"

"They aren't as dangerous in the day, I promise. They can be, if they are provoked or threatened, but they are also curious about people, even friendly. In sunlight they aren't killers without provocation. I suppose if someone pulled a gun on them they might attack, but if you are unarmed and nonthreatening—"

"Ivy," I said. "Listen to yourself."

"You see things so narrowly, Lia. Not everything in the world is a threat."

"But the Watchers are!"

She turned and vanished without responding.

Exhaustion pulled at me. I was too tired to go after her. At least she would be protected from her own foolishness by her blood. And I couldn't control her anymore. She lived apart from us and went where she wanted.

Not everything in the world is a threat.

Sometimes I had a hard time accepting that.

~

"You opened it?"

I stared at the box that lay on Jonn's table, then at the strange devices that had been housed inside. Long, metal shafts protruded from the ends of clear tubes. Inside them, a silver liquid simmered and undulated as if alive.

"What is it?"

"I don't know," Jonn said. Frustration seeped into his voice, and he leaned forward as if he could determine the answer by staring long enough.

I picked one up gingerly and poked the end of the shaft. It was sharp. I winced and withdrew my finger. "A weapon?"

His brow furrowed. "Actually, I don't think so. I've seen something like this before, in a book perhaps." He took the object from me and placed it back on the table in a row with the others. They glittered like knives. A shiver slipped down my spine.

"Should we lock them up again until we figure it out?"

He nodded, absent already, pondering the puzzle as he picked them up one by one and placed them back in the box, where they nestled together on a bed of padding. He flipped the lip shut and put the box beneath his chair. "I'll keep it safe. I'm going to figure out what they are."

I gazed at the box until he covered it with a cloth.

What could they be?

~

"And this," Ivy said, tapping her finger over a large square, "is where the soldiers usually patrol at night."

We all studied the crudely drawn map unfurled on Jonn's table. It depicted Iceless down to the rambling back alleyways and the garbage dump behind the market. I didn't know how Ivy had gotten her hands on such a thing, and when I asked, she said a Blackcoat had given it to them.

I wondered if it had come from the Mayor. If anyone would have a detailed map of the village, it might be him.

"So essentially," I said, "the only way to get into the village undetected is through that weak point in the wall. How are we supposed to move a large number of people inside that way? It would be a tactical nightmare."

"Sister," Ivy said. "You are not thinking creatively."

That comment earned her a glare.

"We have to be clever," she continued. "We have to stop thinking like soldiers and start thinking like sneaks."

"Enlighten me, then."

She crossed her arms. "Think about it. We have a lot of strange faces, as well as some familiar ones who might need a disguise. Lots of strangers, lots of disguises... What's something that might enter the village that meets that description but won't arouse any suspicions?"

"A supply train?" Gabe guessed, looking from her to me.

I shook my head. I knew what Ivy was getting at now. "A traveling caravan."

It was a good idea. Caravans occasionally roamed the Frost, moving between the isolated villages and settlements, bringing letters and news and stories from place to place. They were the bravest among us, the ones who dared to travel through the wastelands amid dangers of snow, ice, and Watchers. Iceliss hadn't had a caravan since the Farthers came. Perhaps it was time for a little diversion. And surely even Raine would be ready for some entertainment.

I smiled slowly. "This might just work."

EIGHT

JONN AND I were in charge of all the weaving for the costumes. Jullia brought us dyes—bright yellows, reds, purples. I taught the fugitives how to make the yarn, and Jonn taught them how to shape the finished product into scarves and cloaks and masks. Ivy helped whenever she was visiting to bring us supplies and news.

"I thought I was done with this cursed weaving forever," she muttered as she worked.

Even Gabe contributed his efforts. He struggled with a bright blue scarf until I took pity on him and assigned him to the task of sorting through the scraps of fabric Jullia had brought us to find pieces large enough to be used for masks and to make patchwork cloaks and dresses.

"Are you sure this will work?" he asked, holding up a piece of red fabric embroidered with blue flowers. "Will Raine let a caravan of traveling performers into the village?" He glanced at Jonn, who was practicing a song on his flute.

"The caravans have always traveled from village to village providing entertainment and bringing letters and news from the other towns," I said. "They are rare here, but cherished. I think even the Farther soldiers might welcome us. But we're going to need to provide that entertainment I mentioned. You don't happen to know how to juggle, do you?"

"No," he said.

I gazed around the room at the fugitives, and I was struck by how few of us there were. This was our army? We were mostly children and young people.

I left Gabe to sort the scraps of fabric and joined Jonn at his table, where he was pouring over some of the medical books I'd brought him from Borde's lab.

"Look at this," he said, shoving the book he was reading at me. "Look."

I looked. Depicted on the page was a black-and-white sketch of a cylindrical object with a sharp, slender line protruding from it. Understanding dawned on me.

"It's the same device as those things we found in the locked box, the one in Borde's closet."

"It's called a syringe," Jonn said. "They were once commonly used to administer medicine."

"Do you think it has something to do with the Sickness? A cure?"

"I thought Borde said there was no cure."

"Well, there wasn't at the time. I have no idea when those things originated. It could have been years after I left."

Jonn nodded, thoughtful. A restless look crossed his face and quickly vanished. "Maybe. But we don't have the Sickness here, do we? So...so it hardly matters. We should just get rid of them."

It seemed incredibly ironic, almost a cruel twist. A cure too late, come to people who didn't need it. But perhaps I could still use this, somehow.

"Well, there's no reason to dispose of them," I said. "They could be valuable. Perhaps someday when we are no longer living in this ruin, a merchant will want them. We could barter with them."

He nodded and resumed reading the book, his brow furrowed. I stared at an empty spot on the table between us, my mind working. Had I really found a cure for the

Sickness? Was it possible such a thing had been discovered after all? Adam had seemed to think there hadn't been one.

But I had other things to worry about at the moment.

"We don't have enough people," I said to Jonn.

"What?"

"For this plan to take back Iceliss. We don't have enough. Look at us." I gestured at the room behind me. "We have a bunch of half-starved fugitives, some of whom are children, most of whom have never seen a day's combat in their lives. How are we supposed to fight seasoned soldiers?"

"Isn't that where the Blackcoats come in?"

I sighed. "Oh wonderful, so in addition we have a bunch of half-starved villagers, most of whom have never seen a day's combat in their lives. I repeat, how are we supposed to fight seasoned soldiers?"

"I suppose the People for the Freedom of the Frost have a plan," he said.

"I sincerely hope so. Or we need to find some other people to help us fight this war." I sighed. "And I need to find a way to contact the Trio."

~

Branches slapped my face as I slipped between the trees. I stopped for a moment and squinted at the path ahead, trying to remember. Trying to picture in my head what the forest had looked like 500 years ago. In my hand, I clutched a rough sketch of the Frost that I'd made with the help of my mother's Frost quilt. I'd drawn marks where I supposed various former Compound buildings should be.

But I only saw wilderness.

75

I stepped around a weathered stone and into a clearing. Snow blanketed the ground. A throbbing blue patch of azure sky showed through the spot where the trees thinned. Rabbit tracks made little dots across the crust of white, the shadows in them a deep blue. The surrounding forest lurked silently, as if the trees were holding their breath.

Based on the location of Echlos and Borde's private lab, the remains of the Security Center had to be around here somewhere. And I was going to find it. It made sense to try all the ruins of the places I knew had previously existed when looking for the way to contact the Trio. Borde's lab had turned up nothing in the vein of what I sought, so I'd moved on.

Something about the landscape seemed familiar, but only faintly. Was this the location of the former Security Center? Everything was bigger, harsher, more tangled. The centuries had gnawed everything familiar apart and grown it back wild and strange.

After a moment of hesitation, I began to cross the clearing. The snow crunched, crusty like old bread beneath my feet.

Then the world gave way, and I fell.

The air punched from my lungs in a strangled huff as I hit the ground. Pain shot through my legs. Snow hissed around me in a cascade. I lay stunned, staring at the sky far above me.

I'd fallen into some kind of pit.

When I could breathe again, I moved my legs and arms. Nothing seemed broken, although everything hurt. I lifted my hands. They were bleeding where jagged pieces of ice had cut them. My back ached, and I tasted blood on my lips—I must have bit my tongue when I fell.

I slid my hands in front of me to get purchase on the ground enough to sit up, and the sound of my movements echoed around me, amplified into something hollow and strange. Groaning, I looked around.

Light slanting through the hole above me and illuminated the space. Thick walls of smooth stone surrounded me, and a corridor stretched away in either direction, the ends veiled in darkness.

The Security Center?

I climbed gingerly to my hands and knees and then to my feet, testing myself for injuries before I stood. My hip ached where I'd fallen, but otherwise I was unharmed. I brushed snow from my cloak and blew hair from my eyes, and then I faced the tunnel. With no light, I was reluctant to venture down it. But how else was I going to get out of here? I couldn't climb back up the way I'd fallen. I couldn't simply wait here, hoping for someone to pass by. This was the Frost. Nobody ventured out into it except Hunters, Trappers, and now Farther soldiers. I didn't dare seek help from any of them.

Sucking in a lungful of musty air, I headed down the corridor.

The back of my neck prickled with every step, but I pushed the thoughts of apprehension away. Fear would not help me now.

The light grew dimmer and grayer the farther I went, until it winked out entirely. No ceiling lights flicked on at my movement—either no power existed in this structure anymore, unlike Echlos, or it wasn't part of the Compound buildings. The ground was spongy beneath my feet, a combination of dust and lichen.

A blue light glimmered ahead. I turned the corner and saw beads of glowing fungi clinging to the wall. I plucked a handful and continued on.

The corridor walls pressed in around me like the edges of a nightmare, hemming me in, keeping me prisoner. The silence-infused darkness was suffocating, and the pitiful light in my hand did little to allay it. Strange, distorted shapes danced in the faint glow that surrounded me. Doorways loomed like mouths of monsters, and shadows dripped down walls and scuttled away from the light like rats.

The corridor dead-ended in steps that twisted upward, and I climbed them, because I wanted to go up. The fungi in my hand cast a soft circle of light around me that touched on the walls and revealed a patch of floor ahead. I turned another corner and paused.

I recognized this hall. I'd spent hours cleaning it. There were the doorways leading into offices and security rooms. Hope blossomed in me. Perhaps this was where Adam contacted the Trio?

My quest to escape forgotten, I searched the offices one by one. The floors were coated in dust, and the furniture that remained had rotted into cadaverous reminders of their former selves. I brushed my hands over the walls and crouched to peer into shadowy corners.

Nothing.

Something about the shape of the final office felt familiar, like the essence of a dream I'd forgotten. I paused, thinking hard. From the depths of my memory rose a recollection of me peering into a room where guards huddled around a glowing box. My heartbeat quickened. Perspiration broke across my back. I stepped into the room and lifted the fungus to see better.

The glint of metal caught my eye, and my pulse stuttered. I took a hesitant step toward the far wall, and the light illuminated a table strewn with humming devices. I sucked in a breath. Was this it?

The pale light of the fungus painted shadows on the wall and threw the devices into garish relief. I saw buttons, tangles of wires, a row of boxes. I ran one finger over the dials and switches and gnawed my lip. How was I supposed to work this thing?

My finger slipped on the dial.

Light shot from the device. The boxes blinked and hummed louder. Glowing words flashed in the darkness.

Agent A, report.

Agent A. Adam? Or Atticus? I reached out to touch the letters, and they swirled away from my fingertips, replaced by rows of new ones all in a jumble. I touched each letter I needed, building a message in return. I kept it brief. I didn't dare say anything about the Blackcoats until I was sure this wasn't some kind of trap.

Agent A gone. Agent L here. Have fugitives. Need orders.

When I'd finished, the message disappeared. I stared for a long time at the blank space where it had been. Was that it? What happened now?

I remained there for a span of hours or minutes, it was impossible to tell. My stomach pinched, reminding me that I hadn't eaten in a long time. My hip throbbed. I needed to get out of here.

The device clicked loudly. I sprang back, startled, as words flashed across the screen once more.

Received. Keep fugitives safe. Gather information. Do what you can to solidify your position.

I composed a reply.

Revolution developing. Instructions?

I waited and waited, but there was no response. Time was slipping away—I needed to get back to Echlos. I decided to return later to see what they'd said.

The machine hummed behind me as I left the room, heading toward where I knew staircases led to the higher levels. I'd never been to those floors before, because I hadn't had permission to see them. But I knew they were closer to the surface, and that was where I needed to be right now.

Ahead I spotted light. The seams of a closed door glowed white. Relief shot through my body. I grabbed the knob and twisted.

The door gave way with a groan of hinges rusty from disuse. I staggered inside, blinded by the light. When my vision cleared, my lungs squeezed and my stomach flipped.

I was not outside. A transparent ceiling—glass?—stretched over me, drenching a massive room of white tile in light.

And in the middle of the room, motionless, were more than two dozen Watchers.

NINE

WATCHERS. NOT FIVE steps away.

I gasped, the sound a harsh rasp in the silence. Every hair on my body prickled as I fumbled for my knife and braced for them to turn at the sound.

But they didn't move.

It was then that I began to notice the small details— the slack positions of their limbs, the glassy black color of their eyes, the stillness of their bodies. They were...dead? Sleeping? Whatever these mechanical things did during the day?

My whole body sagged as relief turned my muscles to mush.

I held still and counted to one hundred, waiting for them to stir. When they didn't, I began to inch backward toward the door. I remembered Ivy's words about their ability to wake in daylight. She'd also claimed they were docile during sunlight hours. Was it true?

The sky, visible through the transparent ceiling, mocked me with its nearness. But there had to be another way out, one that was not fraught with peril.

My fingers closed around the knob behind me, and I twisted it. The door shrieked as I dragged it open, and fresh horror swept over my skin in the shape of goose bumps. But still, the Watchers never stirred.

My courage grew as the creatures remained motionless. I bent and scooped up a piece of debris from the ground, tossing it a few feet from the closest Watcher. The eyes didn't open. The powerful, jointed neck didn't stir. The claws never moved from where they were curled against the floor.

I relaxed. Curiosity sunk its hooks into me, and I let go of the knob and stepped back into the room. I'd never had time to truly study a Watcher in the light of day, and I certainly had never seen so many in one place. They were all different sizes, different colors. Some were black, some iron gray, some pale enough to almost be white. They looked like a pack of ugly, misshapen wild dogs crossed with reptiles, with their too-long necks and too-powerful haunches and curling, talon-tipped feet. Long heads ended in hulking jaws laden with teeth. Spikes lined the necks and descended down backs studded with armored plates and patches of fur. Long tails stretched behind them on the ground. They were terrible, strange, freakish. Monsters.

I raised my gaze from the Watchers to the ceiling. A seam split the glass, and below it...was that a ramp? It was made of metal, rusted but still solid-looking, and it led upward to the seam in the ceiling. I sucked in a breath and crept forward, keeping to the edge of the room. Clearly this was where the Watchers came to sleep during the day, and that ramp must be how they gained access to the Frost at night.

Could I use it to escape this place?

I edged past the slumbering Watchers. How was I supposed to open the ceiling-doors?

But as I reached the ramp, the doors above me groaned and slid apart. Snow whispered down in white granules, bits of ice striking my face and catching in my hair. I breathed in and out in relief and stepped forward.

Then, something behind me moved.

I whirled, my cloak fluttering.

One of the Watchers was stirring. Light glowed in the dark eyes. The claws scraped against the floor, the haunches flexed, the neck swerved. A faint, guttural sound emanated from the jaws.

I hissed a curse and crept backward, fumbling at my waist. Where was my knife? My fingers brushed the handle. I wrenched it out and pressed it to my skin.

The creature turned its head and caught me in its gaze. I stopped as the Watcher rose up to full height.

But instead of red, the eyes were amber. The creature studied me. I remained poised, my finger against the knife, but the creature didn't approach. I noticed a reddish mark on the side of its right shoulder, a streak of paint.

Backing the rest of the way up the ramp, I reached solid ground and fled.

~

When I returned to Echlos, Jullia and Ivy were waiting. Jullia handed me a note from the Blackcoat leaders without a word.

We must meet immediately. Trouble in Iceliss. Give your reply to the bearer of this note along with your preferred location.

I raised my eyes from the note to Jullia. "Trouble?"

She shook her head to indicate that she didn't know. "The soldiers have been more active lately. Nobody knows what Raine is thinking or planning. He's called an assembly this afternoon, and we think he has something he's going to announce. Something important."

I wanted to be at that assembly. I chewed my lip, thinking.

Gather information, the message from the Trio had said.

"I'm going to accompany you to the village."

~

It'd only been a few months' time since I'd seen Iceliss by day, but it felt more like years. Everything about the town was tinged with gray, trampled down, sucked of life. Dried vines gripped the edges of the walls like withered fingers. Dirty snow lined the streets in piles of sludge. Even the sky was the color of cold steel.

The villagers scuttled past with their heads down. Ivy and I joined the flow heading toward the Assembly Hall. I wore a plain, ragged gray cloak instead of my normal Weaver blue, and I kept the edge of it drawn across my nose and mouth to hide my face. But nobody glanced my way, not even the soldiers that stood on every corner.

A crowd had already begun to gather at the Assembly Hall by the time we reached it. I saw a few familiar faces among them. Eyes were lined with shadows, mouths were thin and pressed tightly together, arms were crossed. Everyone looked braced for bad news.

Ivy and I slipped as close to the front steps of the hall as we dared to get, and then we waited. I leaned against the wall and turned my face away from the crowd. Whispers floated around me, snippets of conversation.

"I hear there's been another soldier death due to Watchers..."

"...Wouldn't die if they didn't venture into the Frost like imbeciles..."

"There's been talk of the Blackcoats again. There was a break-in at the Mayor's house...Raine is furious..."

A break-in? I wondered.

Movement flickered at the edge of the crowd, and the people parted like a stream around a rock, the flow of gray and white cloaks cut in half by a stomping retinue of dark-haired soldiers followed by Officer Raine, the commanding officer in charge of the occupation of the Frost. He was smallish compared to the soldiers around him. My chest clenched and my skin prickled at the sight of him. His hair lay in thin wisps over his forehead, his mouth curled in a perpetual scowl, and he lurched with every step due to a limp sustained from an old injury. He looked like someone's grumpy but benign grandfather, not a man bent on wringing every last drop of life from our village. I stepped back so I was clothed in shadows, but he passed by without even glancing my way.

I saw the Mayor, thin and white-faced, following in Raine's shadow, and I wondered briefly what he thought of Ann's absence and the accusations against her. Did he know that his daughter was a member of the Thorns? Surely not. How ironic, how twisted...now he was working with us, and she wasn't here to see it.

I missed her, and the feeling was like a bruise on my heart.

The Mayor and Raine climbed the steps alone and turned to face us as the soldiers fanned out below. Raine frowned at the crowd.

"Quiet," he barked, and the whispers died away to a brittle silence.

He gazed at us coldly. "Word has reached me that the rogue group of idiots—the Blackcoats—are trying to organize trouble again." He spat the word *Blackcoats* like a curse, and a few villagers flinched. Raine stared hard at the crowd, as if daring them to deny it. Then he lifted his hand. Something glittered between his fingers. A necklace?

"A patrol found this in the snow outside the village walls."

Beside me, Ivy gasped. Her hand went to her throat, and she darted a glance at me. Chills prickled my spine. It was hers?

The skin around Raine's eyes tightened. He waved the necklace at us. "There will be a new restriction, thanks to your Blackcoats. If any person is found outside the village without the proper papers—a signed pass from me—he will be imprisoned immediately and sent to the camps."

Dread pooled in my stomach. Jullia. Ivy. They were our message-bearers from the Blackcoats. They brought us food and supplies that helped us survive. If they didn't come, what would we do?

"Do not look at me with those cow eyes," he snarled. "If you people want to keep your precious shops and houses and lives, then you'll do as I say."

"I see you're still seducing them to your side with kindness—a good strategy, I think," a voice drawled from behind us. The words carried easily in the stillness. Heads turned, mouths fell open. Korr. He stood at the back of the crowd, his long cloak fluttering in the wind. Behind him waited an Aeralian coach, the wheels muddy from crossing the river.

Raine's neck turned a mottled shade of red, but he said nothing. Because Korr was a nobleman with orders from the dictator himself, Raine hesitated to speak against him for fear of political ramifications.

Despite my apprehension at seeing Korr, I got a delicious sense of satisfaction watching Raine squirm.

"He's been in Aeralis for weeks," Ivy whispered. "Raine didn't expect him back for some time."

"Will Korr do anything about the edict?" Surely he could see it was utter madness.

"Of course not," my sister said. "But even if he wanted to, he can't. He has no real power here."

"I thought he wanted Frost dwellers to give him information." I remembered how he'd interrogated me before trying to coax me into spying for him.

"He cares only for himself," she said.

Korr smirked and gave Raine an exaggerated bow before turning to go. He didn't even spare a glance at the villagers who stood between him and his political punching bag. Raine whirled and limped in the opposite direction, snapping his fingers to call soldiers to his side. After he'd left the front of the Assembly Hall, the Mayor stepped forward and gestured for our attention.

"Any person who wishes to leave the village and venture into the Frost for any reason—hunting, fishing, trapping, or even reaching your home—must obtain a pass from the Aeralian consulate today. Please, do not test the soldiers on this. They have orders to arrest anyone without the proper documentation."

Ugly mutters filled the air. We needed passes to reach our own homes now?

My heart sunk. How was I going to leave the village? I couldn't obtain a pass. I wasn't supposed to be here. I wasn't supposed to still be in the Frost.

The Mayor shoved his way through the crowd and vanished after Raine. The assembly was over. We were dismissed. Ivy and I left the yard and went into the street.

"What now?" Ivy asked finally, after we'd put several blocks between us and the Assembly Hall. Her voice was doggedly cheerful, but I detected the tremor of worry beneath.

"That was your necklace in Raine's hands. The one our mother gave you as a birthday present two years ago," I said.

She turned her head to hide her expression. "I didn't even notice it missing. It must have fallen yesterday."

"Yesterday? You didn't come to Echlos yesterday."

"Last week, I mean." Her hands trembled as she brushed a tendril of hair from her eyes. "Regardless, how am I supposed to come to Echlos now? Do you think I could obtain a pass on the grounds of checking Da's old traps?"

"You'll have to stop coming until we can figure out a solution. Perhaps the Blackcoats can obtain passes for you."

"What about you?"

"I can try to sneak out now."

We slipped through the center of town, past the market and the shops, past the Quota Yard and the Farther school. It was empty today, and the building silent.

"Where are the children? Don't you have school?"

"We only assemble six mornings a week," Ivy said. "Today, the teacher rests." She made a face as she said *teacher.* I didn't ask.

We reached the edge of the village. The gate to the Frost loomed ahead, bristling with steel and other Farther-built armaments. Ice scabbed the walls and clung in a clouded crust to the edges of the gates. I could see the Cages. The Frost glowed white beyond their bars. My heart surged with hope, but it flickered and died when I saw the Farther soldiers standing guard, weapons slung across their arms.

Still, I could try. I squeezed Ivy's hand before dropping it. I inhaled deeply and approached the gate with an air of confidence.

A gun slapped across my path, stopping me.

"Pass," the soldier said. "I need to see your pass."

"I...I just need to get home. I'll get one tomorrow."

He didn't blink. "No one goes out without a pass, girl. Get it today."

I returned to Ivy's side. We didn't speak as we slipped down a side alley and leaned against the wall behind a stack of barrels.

"What now?" she asked. "You can't stay here forever. Where will you go?"

"We need to contact the Blackcoats. And if all else fails, I can try to slip out tonight through the weak spot in the wall."

"I'll leave a message for them in the normal place, behind the water barrel outside the Blacksmith's shop." She bit her lip. "I've got to get back. They're expecting me to help with quota this afternoon."

They. Her new family, the one she'd been reassigned to. A bitter feeling bristled in my chest. My sister was a Weaver. She shouldn't be working her fingers raw for another family, bringing in their quota and learning their trade. She should be living on my parents' farm, the same as me. She should be weaving...or freely choosing her own path, if she wanted a new one. A wave of determination to see Iceliss free of Farthers surged through me.

"Go," I said. "Meet me here again at six. If I don't come, assume I've found a way out. Don't try to leave the village without a pass. Get one from the Blackcoats if you can't obtain one yourself. I don't want you risking arrest simply to bring us updates about Raine's latest tantrum."

"But the messages Jullia and I bring from the Blackcoats—"

"We will find other ways to communicate with the Blackcoat leaders," I said firmly. "I want you safe first and foremost. Raine isn't playing games."

She frowned, but she didn't argue with me.

"Now go," I said. "Leave the message telling them to meet me here as soon as possible."

"Lia..."

"We'll meet again soon," I promised.

She hugged me briefly, squeezing the breath from me, and then she was gone.

I stood by the barrels for a few minutes, gathering my thoughts and making a plan. For the time being, I was here in Iceliss. I'd better make the most of this opportunity. But I could not be recognized. Fortunately, people tended to see what they expected to see, and no one expected me here. They all thought I was dead.

Perhaps this would be a good time to find out what I could about Ann.

I left the alley and cut through the center of town again. Villagers stood in small clumps, whispering about the new rule and glancing nervously at any Farther soldiers who passed by. No one seemed to see the girl in the gray cloak slipping through their midst. Unnoticed, I passed the bakeries and the smitheries and headed toward the hill where the Mayor's house stood.

The house seemed changed—the architecture was small to my eyes now, harshly white and pitifully plain, a desperate and failed attempt at opulence. Memories of the Compound's glittering, easy beauty filled my mind.

I slipped through the mush of snow covering the garden, heading for the back door. I reached it and raised my hand to knock.

TEN

I HESITATED BEFORE my knuckles touched the wood. This was foolish. I had nothing to say to the servants, who might recognize me, although they didn't know my name. I had no way in.

I returned to the yard. Voices floated on the breeze, and I ducked into the bushes and pressed my back against the wall. Was it soldiers? Had someone seen me?

My eyes narrowed as I recognized the low, silky baritone of one of the voices. *Korr.* I inched along the side of the house until I reached the corner. Bushes shielded me from view, but I could hear everything.

"...A stupid idea to draw the noose tighter around these people," Korr was saying. "You're only going to make them angrier. And angry people do foolhardy, desperate things."

Someone else snorted, or choked, it was hard to tell. Raine? He'd never been good at the witty rejoinders, especially not when it came to certain young Aeralian noblemen who made veiled comments about his limp.

I leaned forward, parting the bushes slightly to see what was happening. There was Korr, standing with his hands on his hips and his dark hair in his eyes, looking spoiled and pretty in his gold-seamed clothing and long black cloak with the purple stripe. Raine faced him, arms crossed, jaw clenched. The Mayor lingered in the background, unobtrusive as a coatrack.

"The Blackcoats are fools, of course," Korr continued. "But they are not without their reasons. And you just gave them another one."

Raine looked about ready to order a firing squad to practice its marksmanship on the young nobleman. His fingers clenched into fists, and a vein in his neck bulged.

"We thought you'd be in Astralux at least another week, my lord," the Mayor interjected, as if desperate to puncture the mounting tension. "Your room is not ready, and I—"

"Miss me?" Korr drawled, turning his head toward the Mayor with a smirk. He looked at Raine again and dimpled. He leaned forward, lowering his voice to a purr as if sharing a delightful secret. "You have to lull these village people into complacency. Have them eating out of your hand, trusting you, needing you. Then they'll give you whatever you want."

"Like you've done with the Mayor's girl?" Raine said.

I bit my lip so I wouldn't make a sound. My stomach twisted. *Done with the Mayor's girl?* What did that mean? What had he done?

Korr stiffened almost imperceptibly, his smile fading and his eyes crackling with sudden fire. Behind him, the Mayor went white.

No one spoke for a moment. Raine's lip curled in a satisfied smile. He knew his barb had hit the mark.

Then Korr smirked again. He straightened, adjusted his cloak, and brushed a speck of dirt from his clothing. "And it worked for me," he said. When he looked at Raine again, his expression was smooth and glib as ever. "Trust me, you're making a mistake."

"I know what I'm doing," Raine growled. "A caged animal will fight back until its will is broken. Then it will simply lie there, and it won't try to escape even if you open the cage door. Believe me, Korr, I have shattered many wills in my life."

Pressure built behind my eyes, the promise of a headache, and I gnawed my lip until I tasted blood. Anger simmered in my blood.

Korr tipped his head to one side. "I don't doubt it. Any brute can break something. It takes finesse to mold and shape it to your own desires."

He turned on his heel and strode toward the house. Raine watched him go with a look of pure loathing. I exhaled shakily and sagged back against the wall. I'd learned one thing, at least. Korr knew where Ann was—and he'd been interacting with her in some capacity.

That gave us a starting place, at least.

I waited until Raine and the Mayor had entered the house, and then I slipped from the bushes and through the garden to the bottom of the hill. I returned to the alley where I'd last seen my sister, taking care to keep my face covered with my cloak.

When I reached the alley, someone was waiting. I slowed, hesitated. A Blackcoat?

The individual turned. It was Jullia. I let my cloak fall away from my face, and she sighed as she recognized me.

"Lia," she said. "Thank goodness."

"Did you get the permit?"

"We couldn't," she said. "Only Fishers and Hunters are being granted them at the moment. There's a list. Your name has to be on the list, or you must put in a petition with Raine. Of course, you are out of the question since we can't explain who you are. We've petitioned for pass, Ivy and me both, but...I'm not sure if we'll be granted them. Since this all just happened today, no one has another solution yet." She rubbed her

93

forehead and peered at me, her expression timid. "What are you going to do?"

"I'll just have to sneak out through the breach in the wall after nightfall." I rubbed my forehead. My head was already aching. "Jonn is going to be frantic. Gabe too."

"We'll find you a safe place to stay until dark," Jullia said. "No one is supposed to be in the streets after sunset, so you can't stay here. Come on."

~

The house was more of an afterthought squeezed between two alleyways, with windows in odd places and a door with a triangular top. Cluttered shelves lined the walls, and a table with six chairs crammed around it stood close to a little black stove.

"You can stay upstairs for now," Jullia said, pulling me toward a ladder that leaned against the back wall. "No one will see you in the attic."

"Whose home is this?" I asked, glancing around with curiosity. Several pairs of ragged socks hung above the stove, drying. Some were tiny. Children's socks.

Jullia looked around as if seeing it with fresh eyes. She licked her lips and cleared her throat. "Mine."

I was unable to hide my surprise. This wasn't the Dyer home, that was for sure—that had been located in the artisans' quarter, and was much larger. And it wasn't the home where she'd temporarily taken up residence with her sister and mother after her father's arrest, either.

She brushed a tendril of hair from her eyes and gave me a tight smile. "I recently married. A widower. He has four small children. He needed a wife. This is his house, and I'm Jullia Butcher now."

"Oh. I...I didn't know." Widower? Four children? How old was Jullia? I couldn't remember. She seemed barely into adulthood. Eighteen?

"My father was arrested. Everiss is gone now." She made a helpless gesture with one hand. "I needed to eat. He needed someone to look after his children. We found a solution for both our problems."

"Does Everiss know?"

Jullia avoided my eyes. "It hasn't come up in conversation yet."

I swallowed my dismay and climbed the ladder. My mind spun, but I reminded myself that this was not so horrible or unusual. Many people in our village married for purposes of advancement or security. But still, rage burned hot inside me. Jullia was barely more than a child. She wouldn't have had to make this sort of sacrifice if Raine hadn't arrested her father to get his land.

Jullia followed me up the ladder and into the attic. A row of beds lined one wall.

"The children stay here," she explained. "But they'll be asleep by the time you leave."

"Does your...does the butcher know?" I was uncomfortable calling him her husband. She was younger than me. When I looked at her, I saw Ivy.

Jullia shook her head. "I was a Blackcoat before I married him. No need to drag him into it." She showed me a large trunk bored with holes. "You can hide here. You should fit comfortably—you're thin enough. See, starvation has its benefits."

Neither of us laughed at her joke. I climbed into the trunk and pulled the lid down.

"I'll bring you something to eat in a bit," she promised, and then slipped away.

The day crept by. I marked its passage by the changing light on the floor, visible through the holes in the trunk. Eventually the light faded, and Jullia brought me a little bread, cheese, and water to consume. Then she left again, and I was alone with my thoughts once more.

The memories of the day were a jumble in my head. Raine's speech, Korr's arrival, his words to Raine about Ann, Jullia's new situation. I tried to sort through it all. Korr was back, but I didn't know why. It seemed that he knew where Ann was...and that he had some contact with her. Rage dug hot fingers into me as I contemplated what he must be doing to her. I remembered his words: *Have them eating out of your hand, trusting you, needing you. Then they'll give you whatever you want.*

With effort, I pushed my anxiety about Ann aside and turned my mind to the other problems. The passes. It would be difficult, if not impossible, for Jullia and Ivy to bring us news about the village now. We'd have to devise a new system for passing information. Perhaps Gabe and I would be making more runs to the village under the cover of darkness.

The clatter of feet on the ladder signaled the children's arrival upstairs. They whispered to each other in the darkness while I measured my breaths and tried not to make any sound. I heard the thump of covers being thrown back, the squeak of bed frames, the rustle of sheets being drawn up around necks. The whispers died away, replaced by steady breathing. All was quiet.

I lifted the lid of the trunk and stood. My legs ached from being confined, and the air outside the trunk was so cold it made the tips of my ears tingle. I placed one foot on the floor and then the other, moving carefully. I paused to listen.

The children's breathing never changed.

I shut the lid and padded silently to the ladder. Easing my weight onto each rung so it wouldn't creak, I descended. The downstairs was dark, silent. A board groaned beneath my foot as I stepped toward the door.

"Who's there?"

A match flared in the dark, and then a lantern glowed, illuminating the space. I pulled my cloak across my face and whirled to face a man with dark hair and vivid blue eyes. He held the lantern high and glared at me.

"Don't move, thief. I'm calling the soldiers."

Jullia appeared, her hair disheveled from sleep. She shot me a wide-eyed glance, pleading for me to let her do the talking, then she laid a hand on the man's arm. "Please. She's a friend. She needed sanctuary, but she was just leaving."

His face softened as he looked at her. He peered at me again. "Go then, and don't come back," he said to me, his tone a warning.

I nodded and went out the door before he could change his mind. My heart slammed in my chest as I stepped into the shadows of the alley and scanned my surroundings to orient myself. I was in the tradesmans' quarter. There was the Baker's shop, shuttered for the night, and across from it I saw the Blacksmith's forge.

The door squeaked at my back, and I turned. Jullia stepped into the street.

"I've spoken to one of the Blackcoat leaders," she whispered. "For now, the plans are all on hold until we figure out a way to work around this latest obstacle. Lie low, and they will contact you when they can."

I nodded. "Thank you. Be safe."

"You too."

She slipped back inside.

Turning the corner, I headed west across the village, straight for the breach in the wall where I'd previously entered and exited with Gabe to meet the Blackcoat leaders. Two patrols of soldiers passed me, but I dodged them both, pressing my back against the rough stones of the house walls and holding my breath until they were gone. When all was clear, I made the run for the wall and squeezed through the narrow opening. The metal slats scraped my shoulders and ribcage, and I felt some of my clothing tear, but I didn't stop to see. Wetness stained my cloak. Blood?

Shouts rang out in the night. Someone had seen me. I kept running, not stopping even when I'd reached the shelter of the trees. Branches slapped my face and dug into my hair. Thorns scratched my cheeks. I slipped on an icy rock and fell hard. I heard soldiers somewhere behind me, but they stopped before entering the woods. They feared the Watchers.

I ran on alone, my heart galloping, my lungs aching with every icy breath I dragged through my parted lips. I ran and ran and ran, splashing through streams and clambering over rocks to hide my tracks so I wouldn't lead the soldiers to the others.

I reached Echlos almost an hour later, soaked from the snow and ice, bleeding in multiple places, and out of breath. As I staggered through the tunnels, a figure darted out of the darkness and grabbed my shoulders.

"Lia? Lia!" Arms enfolded me, squeezing me so tight that I coughed. Gabe. I pressed my face into his neck and shut my eyes.

"I'm all right," I mumbled into his skin, but he didn't hear me.

"We've been looking for you in the forest since this afternoon. Jonn is frantic. He thinks you've been arrested by Raine. What happened?"

"I was stuck in the village until I could sneak out under cover of darkness. Raine passed a new rule that won't allow anyone to leave or enter the village without a permit. I couldn't obtain one, so I was trapped." I leaned against him as we headed for our living space below, and he wrapped an arm around my shoulders. I felt drained of every drop of energy. My legs trembled and my muscles throbbed.

We reached the main room. Eyes turned to us as we entered, and murmurs filled the air. I saw Jonn spot us across the room, and only the way his shoulders relaxed signaled his relief. As we approached, he dropped his eyes to the table and scowled. Everiss was sitting beside him, and she offered me a tentative smile.

I saw a map of the Frost spread across the table between them. Several marks had been made around the village with charcoal. Jonn's fingers were smudged black, and as he rubbed them across his forehead, they left a faint smear.

"Lia," he snapped as soon as we'd reached him. He didn't take his eyes from the map. "You've been gone half a day. We thought you were trapped in one of Raine's jail cells, or worse. We were planning a rescue party. Can't you be a little more mindful of the time?"

"It's not her fault," Gabe said, helping me to a chair. "Raine wouldn't let anyone out of the village without some kind of permit, so she had to wait for nightfall to escape."

"What?" Jonn finally looked up at me, and his eyes widened as he saw my disheveled state. "Oh. Are you all right? Everiss—is there any more of that brandy?"

She went without a word to retrieve it.

I lowered my head onto my arms. I wanted to shut my eyes and sleep for a week, but I needed to tell them everything before I forgot any details.

I recounted the events of the day, from Korr's unexpected appearance to the overheard conversation at the Mayor's house to my evening spent in a trunk in an attic and Jullia's words about postponing the liberation of the Frost until further notice. I didn't mention Jullia's husband.

Gabe straightened with interest at the mention that his brother had returned, and a muscle in his jaw twitched, but he didn't say anything. Everiss returned before I'd finished, carrying a handful of rags and a bottle of brandy. She handed them to me, and I uncapped the bottle and poured alcohol on one of the rags. Gabe took it from me and began attending to the cuts on my arms.

When I'd emptied myself of all explanations, I fell silent. I took one of the rags and joined Gabe in washing my cuts. Jonn leaned back and ran his hands over his eyes.

"This complicates things enormously," he said. "How will we get into the village for the liberation without passes?"

"Like I said, the revolution has been postponed. And we have bigger problems than that at the moment. Like getting enough food now that Ivy and Jullia can't bring supplies anymore."

Everyone was quiet, absorbing these thoughts.

"We'll just have to set more traps, send more people to gather berries," I said. "We'll have to work harder, that's all."

"It's not going to be enough." Everiss licked her lower lip and blinked. Moisture shimmered in her eyes.

"Well, it has to be." I looked at all their faces in turn, daring them to disagree. "We have to make it work. We don't have any other choice. We can't just give up. We'll starve."

"She knows that," Jonn said. He laid a protective hand on Everiss's wrist. "But not everyone is as tough as you, Lia."

Not everyone is as tough as you.

I shoved my chair back and headed for bed.

Gabe followed me. "Lia..."

I sank onto the cot. I was exhausted. Every limb ached. I'd spent the last several hours huddled in a trunk and then running for my life through the Frost without any light to see by.

"I'm flesh and blood just like the rest of you," I said as he sat down beside me. "I'm not made of stone."

He touched my shoulder, and I winced as his fingers brushed one of the places where I'd been cut.

"Sorry," he said.

"No, I'm sorry. I've been harsh, I know. I just..." I shut my eyes. I didn't have words for how wrung out I felt.

"I know," he said simply.

I leaned against him and put my head on his shoulder. He wrapped one arm around me, and we stayed that way until I fell asleep.

~

Every muscle in my body had stiffened by the time I awoke. I stretched, groaned, and muttered curses as I crawled out of bed and stumbled toward one of the fires to warm myself. Memories from the day before swept over me in a black wave, and I dropped my head into my hands. There would be no more food from Ivy and Jullia unless they could obtain the proper permits. Until then, we would have even less than we had now. And we already had almost nothing.

Everiss stirred a pot by the fire. She avoided my gaze.

"What is it?" I asked of the bubbling liquid.

Her curls bobbed around her thin cheekbones as she spoke. "Mostly watered gruel with a little rabbit meat for flavor."

I remembered the tension from the day before. The accusations that I was somehow a creature of unnatural capacity for strength or determination. That I was too hard, too tough. "Everiss..."

"I know we must make do," she said, her voice brittle. "And I will."

"I was going to ask if you would like to help me forage for food tomorrow."

She blinked. She saw the gesture for what it was, an offer of camaraderie as well as a challenge.

"I..."

"If you plan to accompany me, be at the entrance to the Frost tomorrow after noon." I strode away, leaving her staring after me.

~

Later that afternoon, I made the trek alone to the ruins of the Security Center. It wasn't that I didn't trust the others, but I wanted to keep this location a secret. Adam's old reminder came back to me—what you didn't know couldn't be tortured out of you.

I found the entrance of transparent material that led down to the room filled with Watchers. Breathing in deeply, I descended the ramp and confronted the sight of the sleeping monsters.

They didn't stir as I passed them, though every hair on my body prickled in terror. I reached the door and went into the dark hall. This time, I'd brought a lantern. I lit it, holding the light high to illuminate my passage. I hurried through the darkness to the room where the device waited.

The machine hummed to life beneath my fingertips, and a single sentence blinked on the box in response to my question about aiding the Blackcoats:

Do whatever you can.

ELEVEN

I LEANED AGAINST the crumbling wall of the entrance to Echlos, waiting for Everiss and Gabe. The wind teased the tendrils of hair that had escaped my braid. My cloak, the familiar blue one this time, fluttered around my ankles. I chafed my hands to warm them and squinted across the field at the trees. I doubted the Farther soldiers combing the Frost would come this far, but if they did...

A footstep scraped the ground behind me. I turned.

Everiss.

She met my eyes without flinching. She had pulled back her curly mane into a knot at the base of her neck, and she wore one of Jonn's ragged blue cloaks that matched mine. She stepped to my side and surveyed the whiteness before us. "Shall we?"

"We're waiting for Gabe," I said.

She fiddled with the edge of her cloak. "Are you and Gabe...?" She made a gesture with her hand that meant nothing, but I knew what she was trying to say.

"I don't know what we are," I said. "It hasn't been our top priority as of late."

"Love is always a top priority," she said, and blushed.

Now it was my turn to scrutinize her. "What about you and my brother?" The question came out a little sharper than I'd intended.

"He and I—"

But there was a scuffle behind us, and Gabe appeared around the corner. His hair flopped into his eyes, and I noticed the way the sunlight hit the edges and turned them to gold. His mouth tipped sideways in a terse smile. "Ready?"

"Ready," I said, glad to change the subject and get moving. Talking about emotions made me itchy and restless. I didn't know what I felt. There was too much inside my head, and I hadn't had the luxury of sorting it out, not while I was grappling for survival, worrying over my sister, dealing with Blackcoats, and trying to arrange the rescue of my beloved friends.

Or was Everiss right? Was all that just an excuse to delay addressing my feelings?

I pushed all these troublesome ideas into the back of my mind and set out across the snow. Gabe and Everiss followed without a word.

We kept to the tree line but didn't enter it until we'd rounded the edge of Echlos. There'd been a path here 500 years ago. Gabe knew it better than I did, so I let him lead. The path itself was long gone, but the impression of it remained as an old deer run now. Trees twisted overhead and bent close around us.

"Where are we going?" Everiss panted, stumbling behind me as I ducked under branches and yanked my cloak free of grasping twigs.

"We need to check all the traps, and we need to search the woods for berries. Unfortunately for us, Ivy is the one who always knew the best places," I said.

Ivy. Thinking of her filled me with worry. Was she seeking a pass to give her access to the Frost right now? Would she get it? If she was unable to obtain it, when would we see her again?

"I seem to remember there being a lot of berry bushes around the house of the Compound director," Gabe commented. "We should try there."

I remembered that house—an opulent building with sweeping white curves and a roof like a bird's wing. The fields and gardens around it had been filled with snow blossoms—brought here because they were the favorite flower of the director's wife. They'd been bred to withstand extreme cold, and that was why they now bloomed amid our harsh winters.

"It's far from here," I observed. "But all right."

We set out across the wilderness, weaving around massive rocks that protruded from the snowy earth, pushing aside branches laden with ice. When we finally reached the field that led to the house, Everiss stopped and sucked in a breath. "What is that?"

A portion of the house and roof were still visible, covered in vines and snow and shimmering in the pale sunlight like a fallen dove. A swath of blue lay between us and our destination. Snow blossoms. Thousands of them.

"Could this place be any safer from Watchers?" Gabe mused, looking at the snow blossoms in amazement. "This field is literally carpeted with them. They've spread everywhere."

I waded through the sea of flowers. The fragrance wafted around me and tickled my nose.

"Where are you going?" Everiss asked, a hint of panic entering her voice.

"Gabe said he remembered berry bushes growing here," I said. "We need to find them."

"The berry bushes used to grow on the north side," he offered. "Behind the fountains."

"Fountains," Everiss repeated, her eyes wide. "What is this place?"

"It used to be the home of a very rich man," Gabe said.

"Why has no one found it before?"

"Watchers," I said with a short laugh. "Nobody else dares come this far out except crazy and desperate people like us."

As the house grew closer, the details sharpened. The mansion was massive, dozens of times the size of the Mayor's house in the village. Columns covered in lichen and hardened vines stood like sentries frozen in eternal duty. Trees grew through the holes where windows had once been. A ghostly air clung to everything, silence mingled with the sadness of beauty long neglected.

"It's eerie," Everiss whispered. "Have you heard the tales the Trappers tell about the ghosts that roam the far edges of the Frost? Perhaps they live here."

I ignored her. A thought was taking shape in my head. "Do you suppose there could be anything worth salvaging inside?"

Gabe eyed the ruin with skeptical interest. "It's possible, I suppose."

"Inside?" Everiss repeated nervously.

"Cooking pots, tools of some kind..." Excitement caught fire in my blood and propelled me forward. I headed for the first opening I saw. Who knew what wonders might be waiting within this place, preserved from looters all these years by the long distance from the village and a handful of silly ghost stories?

I climbed over a pair of rocks and shimmied up a tree to peer into the closest window-hole. The cool scent of earth—much like the air of a cave—wafted at me. I put my hands on the crumbling window frame and hooked one leg over the sill.

"Lia!" Everiss called after me, her tone frantic. "We don't know what's in there."

"I don't believe in ghosts, Everiss."

She whimpered in response. "Ellis Trapper was *very* sure of what he saw."

I heard the scrape of shoes against bark, and then Gabe appeared beside me, panting. "If you're going in, then I am, too."

I swung my other leg over the sill and jumped.

The fall was short, and I landed on a spongy floor covered in lichen. A hole in the roof let in dappled light, chandeliers dangled from a peeling ceiling, and a pair of marble staircases swirled up to the second floor like the wings of a swan. Trees pushed up through the tiles on the floor and stretched toward the light of the windows. Everything smelled like dirt and stones and secret places. And it was beautiful, this ruined grandeur. Shadows lay over everything, tinting the world blue-gray, the color shifting as the sunlight disappeared and reappeared with Gabe's entrance after me. He tumbled to the ground and rose unsteadily.

Behind us came a few muffled curses, and then Everiss appeared on the window ledge. She blew hair out of her eyes, scowled, and dropped down beside Gabe with a flutter of her cape and a bounce of her curls.

"I'm not staying outside alone," she protested, when we both glanced at her.

"We should look around," I said, and my voice echoed.

I crossed the room to the pair of staircases. I tested one of the crumbling steps with my foot, and thought better of it. Who knew if this place was even stable anymore? I passed the stairs and went down a long hall. Doors opened off either side. I stuck my head into the rooms—they were all the same, hollow gray boxes sprouting with life from the encroaching forest. Trees grew through what had once been windows. Glowing fungi made streaks of blue down the walls. The wilderness was devouring everything inch by inch, year by year. Anything that wasn't stone or some other impenetrable material had long ago succumbed to the elements.

The kitchen was at the end of the hall. It might have been ornate once, but everything was dirty and unrecognizable now. Chunks of the wall had been torn away. The floor was in pieces. I stepped around the bones of a small animal and opened a door in the wall. The hinges screeched. Inside, I found shelves covered in dust.

A pantry. Metal gleamed back at me. Pots, pans. Stacks of them.

"We don't have any food, but here we have lots to cook it in," I said.

Everiss gasped in surprise as she entered the room behind me. "This kitchen is larger than my childhood home."

Gabe reached my side and looked into the pantry.

"Do you remember the things we used to have to eat back then? Piles of potatoes with melted cheese, desserts with cream on them, pork and sauces and fresh fruits..."

My mouth watered. "I remember," I said, feeling a bit faint as the taste of my favorite dessert, apple tarts, filled my memory.

I looked past the pans and saw a dark seam in the wall. "Wait—there's another door here."

"What?" He looked. "You're right."

I pressed my fingers against the seam in an effort to open it. "This is sealed somehow..."

He leaned across me and touched a button recessed into the wall. The door slid aside, and I shot him a look.

"How'd you know that?"

Gabe shrugged. "I did spend several months in that world," he said. "I know how to work the doors."

Darkness lay beyond the doorway. I could just barely see the outline of steps leading down into the blackness. We'd need a light. I returned to the hall where I'd seen the glow fungus and plucked a few pieces. I handed some to Gabe. He took the fungi and balanced it in the center of his gloved palm. I offered a piece to Everiss, and then I turned back to the steps and inhaled the scent of dank underground.

"Let's go."

I listened to every creak and mutter that the building made beneath us as we descended. The steps seemed solid, but still I moved carefully. When we reached the bottom, I felt more tiled floor beneath my feet, this time unbroken and smooth as glass. There was no decay down here, not that I could see. I held the fungi aloft, and a faint glow illuminated the space. Shelves stocked with boxes lined the walls.

Food?

I sucked in sharply. Beside me, Gabe muttered an exclamation beneath his breath. Everiss simply gasped. We all rushed for the shelves at the same time, pulling down containers to see the labels.

"Sugar," Everiss read aloud, her voice cracking. "Honey. Salt. It's a miracle."

"Sausage," Gabe said. He handed the cans to me as he read them. "Beans."

"Do you think they're still any good?" I turned one of the cans over in my hand. Surely 500 years was a long time for anything to last. My stomach tightened with hunger as I spotted a can marked "stewed apples."

"I don't know." Gabe selected another can and stared at it thoughtfully.

"Take as many as we can carry," I said. "And let's get out of here."

"Yes." Everiss's curls quivered as she nodded her head. "Let's."

We filled our sacks with supplies and then retraced our steps to the ruined kitchen above. The light that filtered in through the holes in the walls had turned bluish. The sun would set soon.

"Wait," Gabe said, remembering. "The berry bushes."

~

We headed through the kitchen and down another hall. Gabe kicked away years of growth that had accumulated around a hole where a door had long ago disintegrated. We climbed through it, blinking in the sunlight. The terrace beneath our feet was marble, coated in lichen and ice.

I spotted the bushes first. They grew rampant below the terrace, laden with heavy purple winterberries. A pang of hunger barbed my stomach, and I scrambled down the steps to the landing below. Everiss and Gabe followed, debating the best way to carry the berries back without crushing them all.

We picked until our gloves were stained with streaks like blood, and we ate enough to turn our lips purple. When we'd filled the rest of the sacks, we stopped.

"What's that?" I asked, pointing at the top of what looked like an ice-slicked roof visible just beyond another clump of trees.

Gabe squinted. "I don't know."

I started toward it.

"Lia, it's getting late. The stories..." Everiss began.

I pushed through the wet branches and broke into a clearing with a snap of ice and brittle wood. A building made entirely of what appeared to be glass stood before me. The walls and roof shimmered like ice veined with steel. Frost made delicate patterns across the individual panes. The roof rose into a dome.

Gabe shoved through the brush and stopped beside me. "It's a greenhouse," he said, his exhale of wonder a puff of white in the air.

"A green house?"

"A greenhouse. They're made of transparent material to let in sunlight. They're warm inside. Plants can grow there even when it's cold. We have many of them in Aeralis."

I took a step toward the greenhouse. The sun played across the surface, glinting and sparkling, mesmerizing me. I reached out one gloved finger and touched the glass.

"How has it not been destroyed after all these years?" I said, looking over my shoulder at him. "It's so fragile-looking. Like glass."

"I don't think that's glass," he said. "It's probably something stronger."

I pondered this as I stroked one hand down the slick surface, wiping away the crust of ice. Through the material beneath, I saw a blur of green.

Excitement quickened in my chest.

I rounded the corner of the structure, looking for a door. At the end, I spotted a seam in the wall. I hurried forward, and Gabe followed me.

"The building looks intact," he muttered, half to himself and half to me. "It's really incredible."

Everiss made a helpless sound as she trailed behind us. "I'm not going in there."

"Then wait outside," I said.

I reached the door. There was no knob. I ran my fingers over the seam, searching until my index finger snagged in a hollowed space and the door rushed open with a hiss. Steam swept around us, colliding with the freezing air of the Frost. Gabe and I stepped inside. Everiss didn't join us.

The door slid shut again.

Moisture beaded on my eyelashes and the end of my nose. My feet sunk into grass. I stared.

All around us, sprawling green vegetation pushed toward the ceiling, unruly after centuries of unchecked life cycles. Budding shrubs spilled over a narrow path that disappeared into a grove of trees. The growth obscured my view of the ends of the greenhouse, making me feel as though I'd stumbled into a hidden forest. It was so warm. I pushed back my sleeves and stripped off my mittens.

Gabe reached out and plucked a piece of fruit from a trailing vine. He gazed at it wonderingly. "I can't believe this place remained intact while everything else fell into ruin."

"How is it even possible?" I turned a circle, gazing at the greenery around me. The mysteries of the Ancient Ones' technology were beyond my grasp, yet this seemed downright miraculous.

"Perhaps it was built to supply air and water indefinitely, and it just never stopped. Look." He pointed at vents where air entered the structure, causing plant stalks to wave. "It probably collects melted ice and snow from the roof. Then the water is redistributed inside."

I moved farther down the path. Ahead, I glimpsed a tangle of pipes that sprouted from one glass wall and twisted across the underside of the roof. A fine mist cascaded down from them like rain. "There—the water comes in from there."

Moss covered the path ahead like a vast green sponge, and mushrooms sprouted from it. I crouched down to examine them. They were edible.

"Gabe," I said, my mind working at the implications of what we'd found. "There's food here. Lots of it."

He met my gaze, and his eyes were bright. He held up the piece of fruit. "Shall we go tell the others?"

TWELVE

I SAT ACROSS from my brother, my mouth watering as the scent of stewed winterberries filled the air. I described the places we'd found—the ruins of the house, the cellar filled with canned food, the structure of glass filled with growing things—and he listened to everything.

"Incredible," he said when I'd finished. "And this 'greenhouse' is still intact after all those years?"

"I could hardly believe it. But it's true."

One of the fugitives approached us. I remembered her name was Dana.

"Most of the canned goods are no longer viable," she said, disappointment staining her face. "The salt is still good, and the honey. The beans are, miraculously. The meat is not."

The words sunk to my stomach like stones.

"We still have the berries," Jonn pointed out. "And the fruit and other things you brought from the greenhouse."

"It's a long walk there and back," I said. "We cannot make it every day, not carrying enough food to feed everyone."

"What if we moved our camp there instead?"

I stared at him. "Move to that ruin?"

"And why not? We already live in a ruin. And there is an added bonus—if the snow blossoms are as abundant as you say, then we won't have to worry about Watchers."

"The house is not suitable for living," I said. "It's a crumbled wreck." But even as I protested, I was mulling over what we'd seen earlier. We could live in that cellar, certainly. It would be shelter from the elements. There would be room to spread out, roam, and actually get a little sun. We would be far enough from the village to feel safe for once.

"Perhaps, brother, you've had a brilliant idea."

~

I went with Gabe to examine the location again before we made a decision. We took paper and scribbled a rough map of the rooms, taking note of any areas that provided enough shelter to house people. The cellar where we'd found the canned goods was indeed our best option as a living space, I decided. It was large, secure, and the air was surprisingly warm. There was little ventilation, so fires were not much of an option, but the darkness could be abated with the glowing fungi that grew around the house in abundance.

"And we can cook meals in an actual kitchen," I told Gabe as I surveyed the cavernous space that remained above, complete with ancient cooking devices and a rough stone-tiled floor. "We can build fires here on these stones."

"If only the director's wife could see what we're contemplating doing in her house now," he mused, smiling wryly. "She would have a fit to know someone was cooking food on her fine floors."

"Did you know her?" I asked.

He laughed. "I did work at this house and I saw her around, yes. She was a cold one. Claire and I—" He broke off and frowned at the accidental mention of Claire.

I said nothing.

"Anyway," he said, fumbling for a new topic. "Do we have everything we need?"

"I think so," I said.

He didn't mention Claire again.

~

We moved everyone during the twilight hours between night and dawn, when no soldiers or Hunters would be in the forest to see us. We traveled during a snowfall so our footprints would be covered. Jonn rode astride the gelding I called Officer Raine, and the children rode the mare. The fugitives stayed quiet, staring wide-eyed at the shadowy trees and dripping branches. I walked at the end of the line, scanning the forest for any sign of glowing red eyes, and Jonn rode at the front with Gabe. We were a silent bunch.

The mansion ruins came into view just as the snow stopped falling and the cloud cleared. The sun began to rise over the trees. Rays of golden-pink light touched the tops of the snow blossoms. Murmurs of awe rippled down the line of fugitives, and a few smiles spread across weary faces. Everyone moved a little faster.

Jonn pulled his horse up and let everyone pass him as they followed Gabe toward the house. He and I stayed together at the top of the hill, watching them go.

"It's beautiful," he observed, his tone quiet and thoughtful. "Look at all the snow blossoms. It's like a sea of protection."

I laughed. "Poetic, brother. And Everiss isn't even here to hear it."

As soon as the words left my mouth, I regretted them.

Jonn frowned at me. "We need to talk about Everiss."

"I don't..."

"Lia," he said. "I love her."

"I know."

He turned his head to look at the rising sun. The light caught the edges of his eyelashes and colored them golden. His throat twitched as he swallowed. "I mean, I want to marry her."

My breath left my lungs. "Oh."

"But I wouldn't ask her to marry a cripple."

Anger flared in my chest. "Is that what she said you are? A cripple?"

"No," he said. "That's what *I* say I am."

"Jonn..."

He shook his head. "It doesn't matter now. We have too much else to worry about." With that, my brother slapped the reins across the gelding's neck and rode on, leaving me standing alone on the hill.

~

I made the trek alone through the forest a day later to leave a note in our old living space in case Jullia or Ivy managed to get away from the village to visit us. In it, I told them to leave any food they might be able to bring there, along with notes about how they were doing and any Blackcoat messages they might have to pass along, and I'd be back to check for these things regularly. I left the note secured where they would be sure to see it, then I slipped back toward our new home.

The Frost blanketed me in a sugary dusting of snow. The wind swirled the flakes and made them dance. My mind wandered in circles. We had found a new place to live, and the food there would sustain us for a short while. But I was no closer to discovering where Ann was or figuring out how to rescue Adam than before, and with this new problem of obtaining passes, our plan to infiltrate the village as a caravan had become infinitely more complicated. Furthermore, I didn't know why Korr was here again or what he wanted.

There was much to do, and my looming responsibilities seemed as daunting as walking a tightrope strung across a deep chasm.

~

The wet, warm air of the greenhouse kissed my skin as I stepped down the path, my cloak brushing against waving stalks of fruits and vegetables that grew all around me. Ahead, Gabe carried Jonn to a piece of flat ground, and then Jonn hobbled forward on his own with the aid of his crutches.

I listened to my brother's murmured comments with half an ear as I did my own exploring. The scent of honeysuckle wafted through the air, and fruit dangled above my head like jewels hanging from a necklace. I craned my neck to look at the sun through the ceiling of ribbed glass.

"Do you have any idea what this vegetable is?" I heard Jonn ask as he stopped to examine something.

Gabe had a reply, but I couldn't make it out.

I followed the path farther, through a grove of small trees laden with slender yellow fruit. Something caught my eye. I crouched down and looked closely. The grass beneath the trees was packed down as if a large animal had made its bed there. Had a deer gotten into the greenhouse somehow?

I parted the grass and took a closer look. Shock sizzled down my spine.

A footprint.

Someone had been here, and it wasn't Gabe or me. We hadn't come this far into the greenhouse before.

I fought back the instant panic. Perhaps it was only one of the fugitives. Perhaps they'd wandered inside and decided to luxuriate in the softness of the grass. Except we'd only just arrived, and we'd told them not to go anywhere outside the mansion, not yet.

"Gabe," I said, my voice a shiver in the air.

He rounded the trees. "Are you all right?"

I pointed at the flattened grass.

"I'm not sure what I'm supposed to see," he said.

"Something was sleeping there. Look closer—you can see the shape where it lay. The grass is matted."

He squatted down to examine it. "An animal?"

"There are footprints."

We regarded each other. My heart beat fast against my ribs.

"We aren't alone here," I said.

"Well," he said after a moment. "This complicates things."

~

We met in the cellar with all the fugitives to explain the situation.

"What does it mean for us?" Dana asked, after I'd told them about what I'd seen.

"I don't know," I said. "It's too late for us to go anywhere right now. We'll have to stay here tonight, certainly. I don't know who this interloper is, but they have made themselves scarce for the time being. They appeared to be alone, whoever they are. That's all we know."

"Do they know about us?" Juniper asked from his place at the back.

120

"I don't know."

Everyone muttered and shuffled their feet. I understood their frustration. We were supposed to be safe here—sheltered from Watchers by the snow blossoms, isolated from any chances of discovery by villagers, rescued from starvation by the canned goods and greenhouse harvest. Now, that promise had been pierced by this new and unexpected threat.

I joined Jonn and Gabe by the steps. "We should probably keep an eye on the greenhouse, see if we can catch them sneaking in or out."

"Tonight?" Gabe asked.

"Good idea. We can hide inside. You and I can take the first watch. Jonn, you stay here with the rest. Juniper can help you if you need anything."

A muscle twitched in my brother's jaw. I knew he wanted to stay in the greenhouse with us, but he didn't argue.

~

Gabe and I took up our places behind a row of fruit trees inside the greenhouse that night. Leaves rustled as Gabe settled down beside me and drew his cloak across his body for warmth. I was crouched on my hands and knees, peering at the place where I'd seen the impression of a body earlier.

"Whoever it is, do you think they'll be back tonight?" he asked.

I shifted onto my side and lay down, reluctant to take my eyes off the spot. Grass prickled my wrists, and the smell of dirt filled my nostrils. "It's possible," I said.

Beside me, Gabe's breathing deepened as he began to drift off.

"Gabe?" I asked. He needed to stay awake.

"Hmm?" His eyelids fluttered as he stirred.

"I want you to be in charge of the food supplies. You know where the berries grow, and you're good at giving orders."

"It comes from being a prince," he said, and his lips jerked in a half-hearted smile.

"Well?"

"All right," he said. "I'll do it."

"Thank you." I chewed my lip, pondering all the other things I still had pressing on my mind. Ivy's safety. The Blackcoats' plan to overthrow the village. Jonn and Everiss. And Adam and Ann were still out there, experiencing who knows what. I had to find them. An ache so fierce it took my breath away swept through me, and I exhaled. Gabe's fingers found mine, but I flinched away before I realized what he was doing.

He didn't reach for my hand again.

I let my head fall back, and I stared at the ceiling of glass above me. We were silent.

"Lia?"

"Yes?"

"Never mind." Gabe rolled over onto his back again and folded his arms across his stomach. He shut his eyes.

I kept mine open. I couldn't see the stars through the fogged glass, but I stared up at where I knew they were.

The hours trickled past with the same incessant consistency of the water droplets that fell from the ceiling to water the vegetation. My limbs grew heavy. My eyes turned gritty as sleep began to seduce me. Beside me, Gabe snored softly.

The greenhouse was too dark to see much of anything, but all was silent. Nothing stirred in the blackness. Apparently, our interloper would not be back.

I wrapped my cloak tighter around my shoulders and nestled down to get a little sleep.

That was when hands grabbed me.

I struggled, fought. Voices shouted in my ear. Gabe yelled, but I couldn't see him—everything was darkness and confusion. I swung blindly, and my hand connected with flesh. Someone howled in pain. I jerked away, stumbling, and then I ran.

"Stop! We have your companion!"

I'd reached the door, my fingers grasping for the indention that would open it, but I froze at the command. I turned as a light flared, piecing the darkness, and I staggered back at what I saw.

THIRTEEN

THREE FIGURES ADVANCED toward me, lights in hand. White cloth covered their bodies and faces. I stumbled back, fumbling for something—anything—to use to defend myself. Where was my knife? Had I dropped it in the confusion?

"Wait," one of the figures growled. "Hold up."

The others stopped. I saw Gabe in the background, in the grip of another figure. How had they gotten inside without us seeing?

My fingers finally found the knife tucked in my belt, and I brandished it at them.

"Who are you?" I demanded.

The figure who'd spoken stepped forward and stripped away cloth to reveal a human face. He was a man around my father's age, with bushy eyebrows, chapped red lips, and a coarse black beard.

"I might ask you the same question," he said. "Why are you in our greenhouse?"

Our greenhouse.

My stomach dropped.

"Tell me who you are," I said.

"I'm called Stone. My people maintain this place and eat the food. We have a right to defend it against intruders like you. And defend it we will." His eyes dropped to the knife in my hand. "Are you going to try to fight me with that? Who are you?"

I realized how ridiculous I must look. I lowered the knife to my side. "My name is Lia Weaver."

"Weaver," he repeated. The other figures shifted and looked at each other. "We know about the Weavers."

"What do you know about us?"

"You can walk the forests of this land without fear," he said. "Can't you?"

"I can."

He muttered something beneath his breath and looked at the others over his shoulder. "You're coming with us."

~

They took us out into the night and across the snow at knifepoint. My heart beat fast like the wings of a trapped bird, but my mind was as clear as the sky above us as we passed through the ruined gardens. There were four men. We were outnumbered if we tried to fight, but if we ran...

I tried to catch Gabe's eye, but he was behind me. When I turned my head, Stone ordered me to keep walking. When I ignored him, one of the other men planted a hand between my shoulder blades and shoved me forward.

We left the gardens and passed into the wilderness of the Frost. Trees leaned down around us, twisted and misshapen from the wind. The men moved quickly, their whispers furtive and their glances quick and frightened. I heard the word on their lips: *mechs.*

So they knew what the Watchers really were?

We passed from the forest into a flat wasteland where no trees grew. Rocks jutted toward the stars, their edges glittering with ice. Wind howled around us, making our cloaks dance and flinging shards of snow at our faces. Stone wrapped the cloth back around his mouth. Gabe and I suffered along with nothing but the edges of our cloaks to shield ourselves.

Finally, I saw light.

Beautiful, transparent sculptures rose out of the darkness, statues of animals and men. As we drew closer, I realized they were carved from ice. Beyond them lay what appeared to be a village of tents.

"This way," Stone said, leading us down a lane that ran straight through the forest of carved creatures. Although it was night, people moved freely among the sculptures and the tents beyond. I saw children playing tag around a fire.

"Aren't you afraid of Watchers?" I asked. "It's night."

"Watchers?"

"I mean the monsters," I said. "Mechs."

He shook his head. "They don't come this far. They turn away before the wastes. It's the end of their territory, and they never cross the line."

I absorbed this information. So this was the end of the Compound land, then.

"Come on," Stone said, pointing toward a camp of tents set in a cluster. A wall of ice blocks encircled them, shielding them from the wind. We had no choice but to go where he'd pointed.

I heard a wavering trill of music. Flutes. It made me think of Jonn, and my chest ached with sudden fear. When would the others discover we had gone missing? What would they do?

My family was splintered—Ivy stuck in the village, Jonn back at the mansion ruins, and now I had been taken prisoner and forced to journey to who knows where. My stomach twisted, and I felt like vomiting.

We reached the tents. Stone thrust aside the flap of the largest one and put a hand on my shoulder, propelling me firmly through the doorway and inside.

Warmth hit my face and made my cheeks tingle. The flicker of firelight lit the space around us. A few people sat around the perimeter of the tent, and a woman tended the fire in the center. Her long hair glittered reddish gold where it spilled over her shoulder. My heart skipped a beat—Claire?—but then the woman raised her head to look at us, and her face was unfamiliar.

"Sit," Stone ordered, and I let my legs fold beneath me. I sank onto a pile of animal skins and stared up at our captors. One of the others shoved Gabe down beside me, and he found my hand with his and squeezed. We exchanged glances, and I read the question in his eyes.

I shook my head slightly to indicate that we should do nothing. Not yet. I had no idea where we were, it was nighttime, and Gabe didn't have any snow blossoms even if we did make it back to the Frost. There was no sense in running until we'd tried to talk, and we couldn't fight. We were outnumbered many times over.

Stone crossed the room to the fire and drew a pot from the coals. He poured steaming liquid into cups and returned to us. He thrust one at me and handed the other to Gabe. Then he left the tent.

I inhaled the steam from the cup, and the scent of mint filled my nose and made my throat prickle.

The red-haired woman spoke. "That will warm you. It's cold out tonight."

She was expressionless, but her eyes brimmed with curiosity as she gazed at us.

I took a sip, and the liquid made a trail of fire down my throat and burned in my belly. I coughed.

"What do you think they're going to do with us?" Gabe asked, his voice barely a whisper.

"I don't know. They know my name—Weaver." My stomach turned over as I said it.

"Do you think they want something from you?"

"I don't know... I even don't know how they've heard of my family. I've never heard of these people before. I didn't know they existed."

Time slipped past. The woman tended the fire. My eyes began to feel heavy, and I struggled to stay alert.

The tent flap moved, and Stone reappeared with another man beside him. I saw the knife in the man's hands, and I scrambled to my feet. A man and woman appeared at my side. One pushed me onto my back and the other grabbed my shoulders to hold me in place. I kicked, thrashed, but my head was spinning and my muscles felt limp and tired. The drink—had they drugged me?

"Lia!" Gabe shouted. He tried to push the hands away, but more people surrounded us, and then they were dragging him back while the others held me down. I heard the sound of a fist striking flesh, and Gabe moaned.

The man with the knife bent over me and pulled my arm taut. He opened my sleeve, bearing my skin. The blade flashed in the firelight.

"No," I gritted out between clenched teeth.

The edge of the knife opened my vein, and rich red slid in a stream down the white of my arm. The man pulled a glass tube from his belt and pressed the edge against my arm, catching the blood. My arm throbbed. My heart thudded in my chest. Sweat prickled across my neck and back, and nausea swept over me.

The man capped the first tube and produced a second one.

My vision dimmed. The hands that held me in place were too tight. The ground beneath me dug into my back, and my arm was so cold. I stared at the place where my blood welled up as vomit rose in my throat. Would they bleed me dry?

"Enough," Stone said, and the man with the tubes stepped away. Stone knelt beside me and wrapped my arm with a piece of cloth. He pressed his thumb against the cut and bent my arm at the elbow, keeping pressure against it. "Let her up."

I struggled into a sitting position using my good arm. Across the room, I saw Gabe on his knees, flanked by two men, his hands and feet tied with rope and his right eye swollen from where he'd been hit.

"Drink this," Stone said, putting more of the mint-scented drink into my cup and offering it to me.

I glared up at him. "You think I'm falling for that again?"

He looked ashamed. "It will make you feel better. You're too weak. You're underfed—"

"If you're so concerned with my health, perhaps you shouldn't have forcibly bled me."

He put the cup down by my hand. I moved my fingers away from it even though my throat ached with sudden thirst.

"We need to talk," he said.

"What more do you want from me?" I was angry, but almost instantly, I regretted the outburst. I needed to be cool, calm, calculating. I needed to talk my way out of this instead of snarling and crying like a fox in a trap.

"Let us be alone," Stone said firmly, without taking his eyes from mine.

Without a word, the others rose and headed for the tent flap. The man who'd taken my blood vanished with the rest. They left Gabe, still tied hand and foot, at the other end of the tent. His eyes met mine across the empty space, and I saw the violence in his expression. I shook my head. We needed patience now. We needed to bargain.

Stone sighed. "I'm sorry. I did not want them to do that. But I couldn't convince them that—" he stopped.

"You couldn't have *not* kidnapped me?"

He ignored that comment. "As a Weaver, your blood is very valuable to us. It's possible it saved your lives tonight, as there are those who wanted you, a stranger who was in our greenhouse, dead. I'm sorry for what happened, but you should be grateful."

"Grateful? You kidnapped us, brought us here against our will, and bled me. And I'm supposed to be grateful you didn't kill us, too?"

I was getting too angry. I sucked in a deep breath to calm myself.

Stone rubbed the space between his eyes. "You were trespassing. We have a right to defend ourselves against interlopers."

I wanted to argue with him, but I needed to focus. "What happens to my friend and me now?"

"I'm not interested in keeping prisoners," he said. "So I'm hoping we can come to an agreement."

"An agreement? How?"

He didn't respond. He just studied me.

"Well, I have a few questions. Who are you people?" I looked around the tent at the furs, the open fire, the metal pot.

"We don't have any formal name, but we call ourselves the Wanderers. We never stay in one place for too long. We follow the deer."

Hence the tents, I supposed. "How do you know about my family?"

"My ancestors lived here before the Great War," Stone said.

"The Great War?"

130

"The one that followed the Sickness. They were trying to find a cure here, in a place called the Compound."

"I've...heard about that."

Gabe choked on a laugh at my understatement. Stone ignored him.

"They didn't succeed. Society disintegrated, and the work here was abandoned. Our forefathers had to flee beyond the Compound boundaries because of the creatures that guarded it, the mechs. They turned wild and attacked everyone. Everyone but your ancestors."

"And how do you know all this?"

He eyed me. "I only know what I've been told by the stories. There were always rumors of a family living within the remnants of the Compound near the Iceliss village, a family who could roam the snowy wastes at night without fear."

I was silent.

"Life is harsh here, but safe. My father's generation lived in the warmer regions, but when I was a boy we were driven north by the Aeralians." He spat the word. "Hateful people. Half our numbers were lost."

"The Aeralians occupy the Frost now," I said. "They occupy my village."

"Yes, I've heard of soldiers in the woods. I hear the mechs got a few of them."

I nodded slowly. "They've built walls now, fences. They're frightened of the monsters."

Stone grinned at that, but his smile faded as he looked at me again. "And your people, what has happened to them?"

"The occupation is killing us. We are starving."

He reached out and ran a finger down the side of the cup of drugged liquid he'd tried to get me to drink. "My people hunt and trap, but many of the animals move

131

into the land we dare not enter as the spring approaches. We are often hungry. With vials of your blood, we could enter the Compound again."

"There are things besides my blood that repel the monsters," I said.

He raised his eyebrows. "We know little about them, except their true nature."

"And yet you know my name."

"There was a man," he said. "He told us about you."

"A man?"

"Yes. He came to us heavily wounded, accompanied by a companion. He was sick. He rambled in his sleep, talking of Weavers and the monsters and blood. Some of my people thought he was a prophet."

"And you?" My heart beat fast. Who was this man who spoke of my family?

"He was just a man," Stone said. "A man with knowledge."

"And his name?"

"He didn't give one. He didn't stay with us long. We called him Scar, for he had many after he'd healed."

My mind spun with questions.

Gabe spoke up from across the room. "What happens to us now? Are you going to keep bleeding Lia until you've killed her?"

"My people want access to the Compound again," Stone said. "We are facing another long summer without good hunting, and I'm afraid some immediately saw you as the solution to that problem."

"There are other ways to gain access," I said again. "I could teach you them in exchange for our freedom."

"I will speak with the leaders. They'll decide what to do with you." He started to rise.

"Stone," I said.

He paused.

"I am part of a plan to drive out the Aeralians," I said. "If we succeed, the Frost will be ours again. No more Farthers. Isn't that what you want? If you don't free me, it might not happen."

He studied my face as if looking for signs of duplicity. "I will mention this to the others," he said finally. "They might find it worth considering when it comes to your fate."

Reaching into his pocket, he produced a rope and bound my hands behind my back. I winced as the movements jarred my throbbing arm, and Stone noticed. "I'm sorry," he said. He got to his feet. "I'll have someone bring you some food."

With that, he vanished through the tent flaps, leaving us alone.

"Lia," Gabe growled, wriggling toward me on his knees. His hands and ankles were both bound, which kept him from standing. "We have to get out of here before they decide to tap your veins until you've been drained dry—or keep you here forever as some kind of blood slave." He reached me, panting, and looked at the knots in my bindings. "Perhaps if we put our backs to each other, we can undo these ropes—"

"Not yet," I said.

"What?"

"Listen. If we can get these people on our side—and they have every reason to want to be—we have that many more to assist us in liberating the Frost."

Gabe blinked. "You think you can trust these people after what they've done?"

"They've done what they've done because they're desperate."

He looked at my bandaged arm, and his meaning was clear. Could I trust them not to get desperate again?

I wasn't sure that I could, but I had to try.

133

~

The red-haired woman who I'd mistaken for Claire earlier returned with a pitcher of drink and a platter of charred meat. She set the food before us and started to leave.

"How can we eat with our hands bound?" Gabe demanded.

I looked at him sharply. Was he planning something?

The woman paused and tipped her head to one side, glancing him over as if trying to determine how likely he would be to escape. Gabe looked back, his expression blank.

"I will untie your hands," she said. "But only so you can eat. Then, they will be rebound, do you understand?"

Gabe nodded. She crossed the room again and knelt before us. Her cold fingers brushed against mine as she undid my ropes, and I wiggled my hands and stretched my arms to get the blood flowing again as soon as I was free. A dark stain had seeped through the bandage on my arm.

The woman freed Gabe's hands and stepped back. A knife glittered at her belt in the firelight as she moved.

"Eat," she said, fingering it.

We reached for the meat. Hunger was suddenly tearing its claws into the walls of my stomach, and I chewed with savage enthusiasm.

Gabe ate slower. His eyes darted around the room, resting on various objects, lingering on the doorway. He leaned close to me and spoke in a whisper. "We need to make our move now. We're nearly alone, we're untied..."

"No," I said. "I want to talk to Stone again."

"Lia—"

"Eat," the woman commanded, and he bit into his food.

I reached for the bread and tore off a piece.

Gabe dropped his bread between his feet and muttered a curse. He hunched over to retrieve it. "My hands are clumsy from this cold," he said, looking at the woman as if it were all her fault.

She sniffed in derision.

When we'd finished the bread, she approached us to retie our bonds.

"Wait," Gabe said. "I need another drink."

The woman offered him the pitcher. But instead of taking it, he hurled the liquid into her face. She staggered back with a howl of pain as the hot drink splashed in her eyes. Gabe leaped to his feet.

"Come on, Lia!"

He'd undone the ropes around his ankles when he'd pretended to drop his bread.

"Gabe—"

Footsteps pounded outside. My feet were still bound. I looked from the ropes to his face.

Gabe stepped back. "I'll tell the others. We'll come for you."

And then he ducked through the tent flap and he was gone.

FOURTEEN

CHAOS FILLED THE tent in Gabe's wake as people rushed inside armed with spears and knives. Hands grabbed me. The woman with the burned face shouted and pointed. Blisters covered her cheeks, and the front of her garment was wet. She glared at me as someone bound my hands again.

Stone appeared, yanked me to my feet, and dragged me outside. Cold wind whipped my face and swirled beneath my cloak, chilling me. The torches cast golden circles around us, and snow was falling, a gentle swath of white amid the confusion. My ankles were still tied, and I stumbled a few feet before he bent and picked me up.

Armed men spilled past us, heading for the open darkness beyond the tents. I didn't see Gabe anywhere. A strangled feeling filled me, threatening to choke me. What would they do when they caught him?

Stone carried me to another tent, a smaller one with no one inside it. He dumped me down on a pad of furs and paced to the doorway. "Stay there," he ordered.

I struggled up into a sitting position. "What's going to happen to him?"

Stone just shook his head.

I fell back. The room spun, and nausea crawled in my throat again, but I didn't vomit. I lay still, staring at the top of the tent and watching the way the shadows of the people running outside danced across it.

"Stone," I said aloud.

He looked at me but didn't speak. His face was a riot of anger.

"You have to let me go. Gabe will get away, and he will find my people. They'll come for me. They'll fight you. Do you want that?" My heart beat fast as I spoke. My threats were a gamble, but what other choice did I have?

"No," he said. "But if we catch him, they won't know where you are, so it won't matter."

"They'll look for us. They'll find us." But I wasn't sure if that was true—the finding part, anyway.

Stone didn't reply.

I was still, waiting for sounds of Gabe's capture, waiting for my hopes to fall. But they didn't come. Silence filled the air. I counted seconds, minutes. Time slipped by in little eternities. My breathing slowed. My eyes grew heavy with the exhaustion that followed panic.

Footsteps crunched in the snow, and a shadow painted the side of the tent in lines of gray. "He escaped across the boundary," a voice reported. "We did not chase him beyond it."

Stone swore and turned to look at me. I lifted an eyebrow.

He sighed. "Speak your piece, then."

"My people have supplies," I said. "Things you could use in exchange for our shared use of the greenhouse. We have knowledge of the Frost—the place you call the Compound. We have knowledge of the Mechs. If you make a peace agreement with us, we can share these things with you. If you do not, we might have to fight you to ensure our survival. Do you really want that?"

He was listening.

"Please," I said.

"I will speak with the others in the morning."

~

At first light, the leaders deliberated. I waited outside the largest tent in the circle, huddled on a stool covered in fur, bundled in my cloak as I strained to make out the low murmurs inside. A young man with long red hair and a scraggly beard waited with me, unmoving and unspeaking. The wind blew my hair into my eyes. I tasted thawing snow on the air.

The world around me looked different by the pale light of morning—sadder and less vicious. The ice statues dripped in the sunlight. Fire pits smoldered, releasing curls of gray smoke toward the sky. The tents seemed small and ragged, huddled against the cold like shivering children.

"What are those statues for?" I asked my guard.

He looked at me, his eyes flat and cold, and for a moment I thought he would refuse to reply, but then he said, "They are carved to remember our dead. We etch them fresh from the ice at every campsite, one for each family who Wanders."

I ran my gaze over the people—children playing with small stones in the snow, men and women working at tanning racks or tending fires. Everyone wore simple, thick clothing made of animal skins. Both men and women wore trousers. Their long hair—which came in shades of red, brown, and black—was bound back in tails with strips of cloth that hung down their backs. Tired eyes and unsmiling mouths regarded me with open suspicion. Accounts of hard work were scribbled across their sun-chapped faces, and sorrow was etched deep in every line on their brows.

The Frost was not the only harsh place in our world, it seemed.

Finally, the murmur of voices ceased, and Stone emerged from the tent. He dismissed my guard and reached down to unbind my hands. "They have agreed that you can go," he said, without any preamble.

"And the greenhouse?"

"They have also agreed that your people may share a portion of it, in exchange for the information and supplies you mentioned. I will meet you at the greenhouse for these exchanges. I will come for them in two weeks' time. Do not even think of cheating us in this bargain. We are not to be trifled with."

Stone gave me directions back to the greenhouse and a canteen of fire-warmed water to carry with me. We said no goodbyes. I turned and headed across the white wasteland, following our line of footprints from the night before back across the boundary line and into the Frost.

~

I moved slowly because of my weakness from being bled, reaching the mansion ruins by midmorning. I climbed the crumbling steps to the great house. When I slipped inside, the echo of frantic voices emanated from one of the rooms off the kitchen.

"Well, we have to do something!"

I recognized the voice as Gabe's. Relief shivered through me. He'd made it back, then. No Watchers had gotten him. He hadn't lost his way.

"Of course we're going to do something, don't be insane. I won't leave my sister to be bled out like a slaughtered animal at the hands of—" Jonn broke off as his voice cracked. "I'm only saying that we have to be smart about it. We don't have the numbers or the weapons to rush in and fight them. I need to contact the

Blackcoats. Maybe they can help us." He fell silent, and I heard the scrape of feet and the creak of crutches. He was pacing.

I moved down the passage toward the sound of their voices.

"Do you think she's all right?" I heard my brother ask, and he sounded utterly broken.

"She's strong," Gabe said. "She's a fighter."

"She'd better not do anything stupid in the name of bravery."

"When have I ever done any such thing, Jonn Weaver?" I demanded, appearing in the doorway.

They both whirled in astonishment.

"Lia!" Gabe crossed the room in three strides and pulled me into a bear hug.

Over his shoulder, I saw Jonn sag against his crutch. His eyes fluttered with relief, and he flashed me a sheepish smile. "You weren't supposed to hear that, but I am glad you were here to do so. Are you all right?"

"I'm all right," I said, the words a sigh. "I'm here and in one piece."

Gabe released me and pulled away to look at my face. "What happened? How did you escape?"

"I didn't escape. After you left me, I made a bargain with them."

"Left you," Gabe repeated, catching a whiff of my anger.

"A...bargain?" Jonn's expression turned apprehensive.

"Don't look so worried, brother. I've negotiated our use of the greenhouse and I may have made some new allies."

I explained the deal I'd made with Stone. Gabe scowled, but Jonn looked thoughtful.

"This may be difficult, but it might come in handy. Good work, sister. You're becoming a diplomat. Ivy won't believe it."

Ivy. Thinking of my sister made my stomach twist. "Has there been any word from her, or anyone else in the village?"

"No one has made the journey back to Echlos to check," Jonn said.

"I'll go." At the moment, I was angry with Gabe and I needed to sort it out. Walking was the best way to think these days.

"You need to rest," he argued. "You look ready to drop."

"I'll eat something, and then I'm going."

"Lia..."

He looked so worried that I recanted. "Tomorrow, then. But I want to be the one to go."

I turned and left the room. I wanted my cot and a warm blanket and nothing else for as long as possible.

"Lia." Gabe caught up with me and snagged my arm, whirling me around to face him. "I...please talk to me."

"What is there to say? You decided to run, I didn't. You left me there alone."

"You're angry."

The corners of my mouth turned down. I didn't know how to quantify how I felt. His move had made sense, and I understood it logically...so why did I feel so betrayed?

I pressed a hand over my eyes. "I need to sleep. We can talk about it more later."

He let me go.

~

Late afternoon had painted the forest golden and purple by the time I reached Echlos the next day. I crossed the plain toward the familiar white rounded roofs, smooth as eggshells against a cloudless blue sky. I would leave another note explaining that if we received no new word in a few days, I would sneak into the village and knock on Ivy's door myself. We needed to make contact with the Blackcoat leaders again, and I needed to make sure my sister was safe.

A shadow flickered at the edge of my periphery, snagging my attention. I stopped just inside the entrance to Echlos. A skitter ran down my spine as my senses prickled with awareness.

Someone was here.

Ivy?

I couldn't be sure, so I stepped back and pressed myself against the wall, waiting for the other person to make the first move. My heart pounded even though the likelihood that it was a solider was almost nonexistent.

"Hello?"

The voice echoed, a hesitant whisper in the silence. I sighed. Jullia.

I stepped away from the wall to meet her. "It's Lia Weaver."

She was at the end of the hall, near the steps that led down to our former dwelling place. She turned at my words and hurried toward me.

"Oh, Lia. I thought... I couldn't find any of you..."

"I left a note," I said.

"Yes, I found it, but..." she broke off and moved her hands in a helpless gesture. I noticed her eyes were red-rimmed and her face was the color of ash.

"Are you ill?"

She laughed, a hysterical sound. "I'm fine. It's...it's Ivy."

142

The mention of my sister's name pierced me. I went still. "What happened to Ivy?"

Was it Watchers?

Jullia covered her face with her hands and sucked in a deep breath. Her shoulders rose and fell.

"She's been arrested."

FIFTEEN

"ARRESTED?" I HISSED, sure I must have heard her wrong.

Jullia nodded.

I sagged back against the wall, my whole body turning numb as I absorbed the news.

"She was trying to sneak out to see you," Jullia said. "We never were able to get any proper passes to leave, you see, so she went through the secret way in the wall. The soldiers found her when she was halfway through the forest. They were on one of their patrols. They brought her in, and locked her in a cell." She sniffled and wiped at her eyes. "What will we do?"

Certainty steeled me. It made me resolute and deadly calm.

"We're going to rescue her," I said.

~

We moved under cover of darkness, a party that included Gabe, Juniper, and me. We wore black scarves over our faces. We didn't speak as we crossed the forest and fields of the Frost, heading for the village.

The plan was simple: get in, get Ivy, get out. One of the Blackcoats would be waiting to meet us just inside the walls, and he or she would give us more information. We would proceed from there.

We reached the top of the hill that looked down on Iceliss and paused in the shelter of the trees. Below us, the village gleamed the color of ice and bone in the light of a full moon.

"We have to be careful that we aren't spotted as we cross the snow to the wall," I said to the others. "It's bright tonight. Stay as close to the shadows as possible, and cross the shortest gap between the trees and the walls."

Gabe and I hadn't resolved our differences regarding his leaving me with the Wanderers and escaping alone, but there was no malice between us tonight. There couldn't be. Ivy was in danger and every fiber of my being was focused on rescuing her.

"Let's go."

We crept down the hill, keeping to the shadows. When we reached the edge of the field that separated the village wall from the forest, we paused to divide up. Gabe and Juniper went first, skirting the perimeter until they'd gone as far as they could without crossing the blank stretch of white, then they were two fluttering shadows in the night as they darted across the field.

I waited until they had reached the safety of the far side and then I started after them.

Light flickered on the wall. A soldier lighting a match. His back was to us. I ran across the snow with my heart in my throat.

Almost there.

I reached the weak place in the wall and followed the others through the space between the cold pieces of metal. On the other side, a piece of darkness detached itself from the shadow of a house and slipped forward to meet us.

The Blackcoat.

"Bluewing?" a gruff voice asked.

"Here," I said, stepping forward. My face was hidden by my scarf.

The Blackcoat pressed a roll of paper into my hand. "Here are the instructions for her rescue. She's in the holding cell inside the Farther offices."

"Thank you. We'll be in contact soon," I said. "I'll have someone meet you in three days."

The Blackcoat nodded and vanished down the alley, leaving us alone. I unfurled the paper and found a scribbled set of instructions.

The key to the holding cell is located inside the third room of the Farther offices. Be sure to replace it to stall detection. The holding cell itself is in the sixth room on the right. You will gain entrance through the back door, which is guarded. It is unlocked, and the guard will be away for ten minutes between the changing of the guard at midnight. This is your only chance, so move quickly.

I lifted my eyes from the paper to scan the half-hidden faces of the others.

"Let's go."

~

We found everything just as the note described. A guard leaned against the frame of the back door, smoking. The cig glowed like a star in the darkness, and when he exhaled, the smoke mingled with the white puff of his breath.

I pressed my back against the wall of the house behind me and motioned for the others to wait. Somewhere, a dog barked. The wind whispered over the street and fanned our faces, and far away, I heard the clatter of boots against stone as a patrol passed by. The tension threatened to strangle me. Was my sister all right? Would this soldier leave as the note had promised? What if we couldn't find her, couldn't free her?

Just before the Farther clock in the village market clanged to announce midnight, the soldier straightened, flicked his cig onto the ground, and vanished down the alley.

"Now," I whispered.

We found the door unlocked as the note had specified. Gabe and I slipped inside while Juniper lingered on the stoop, keeping anxious watch.

The office rooms smelled of dust and furniture polish, and an underlying scent of fear and danger clung to everything like smoke from the soldier's cig. My blood thrummed in my veins, beating like little fists at the pulse points in my wrists and neck.

"This is a little different than last time, isn't it?" Gabe muttered under his breath as we crept down a dark hallway, counting the doors.

I didn't reply. My voice had dried up.

We stopped at the third door and I turned the knob. The floorboards creaked beneath our feet as we entered a study lined with shelves and cabinets. I scanned the darkness, looking for any glint of metal.

"Where's the key?"

I searched the desk while he examined the shelves. I found nothing but papers and a couple of empty whiskey bottles in a drawer.

"Here it is," Gabe whispered, snatching the key from a ring behind the door. "It says 'holding cell.'"

We went back into the hall. I struggled to breathe as we crept down it, stopping at the sixth door. It was metal, with a slot for food near the bottom. I nodded at Gabe, and he inserted the key and twisted. I yanked the door open as soon as the lock clicked.

"Ivy?"

She was just a tiny shape huddled in the far corner, her face a scrap of white in the darkness.

"Lia," she whispered. "It's you."

She was well enough to speak, at least. I exhaled. "We're going to get you out of here." I crossed the room to her side and felt for chains. It was too dim to see much.

"I'm not bound," she said.

"Then let's go." I grasped her hands and pulled her to her feet. She leaned against me, and I wrapped one arm around her shoulders. Leaning together, we headed for the cell door where Gabe waited for us.

"Gabe?" Ivy asked uncertainly, peering at him in the gloom.

"It's me," he said. "You're safe now, Ivy. Don't worry."

She nodded and nestled her head in the crook of my shoulder. I squeezed her tighter against me, wanting to be sure she was safe and solid and in one piece.

We went out into the hall, Ivy with me, Gabe relocking the door behind us and then hurrying ahead to replace the key in the room where we'd found it. My sister and I reached the door to the outside and met Juniper on the stoop. There was still no sign of the soldier yet, but we had to hurry.

"Can you run if it comes to that?" I asked Ivy.

She nodded again, and I gently freed her hands from around my waist. "Then be ready to do so if I tell you. We might have to move quickly if the soldiers spot us."

The wind swirled around us as we exited the building. Ivy had no cloak, and she shivered. I draped mine around her shoulders and tugged her close, sharing my body heat with her as we walked. "Come on. If we move fast, you'll be warmer."

We slipped down the alley and into the street, heading for the point in the wall where we could make our escape. The sound of our feet against the cobblestones matched the thudding of my heartbeat. Darkness painted us invisible. We turned the corner and passed the Assembly Hall. My eyes traced the familiar shapes of the windows and doors, the carvings of snow blossoms. Everything seemed harsh and strange now, like memories filtered through a nightmare. Behind us, I heard the clip of soldiers' boots as a patrol drew near.

"Hurry," I whispered.

We reached the wall and followed it to the gap. Gabe went through first, his cloak slithering after him and his heels scraping the slats. Ivy followed him. Juniper looked at me.

"Your turn," he said.

I shook my head. "I'll go last."

He didn't argue. He squeezed through the narrow opening like a fox through a fence.

I took a moment to glance behind me, to make sure that no one had followed us. The alleyways were silent. A puff of wind stirred my hair, and the shadows flickered. My heart stuttered—was someone there? But at second glance, the movement was only a piece of curtain fluttering in a window.

I ducked through the gap in the wall and followed the footprints of the others toward the trees.

~

I dug up one of the supply parcels that Adam and I had buried months ago, and took the cloak that wrapped the other things. I shook off the bits of dirt that remained and draped it over Ivy's shoulders. Snow fell gently around us, bathing the world in redemptive white. It gathered in Ivy's hair and caught on her lashes.

"Thank you, Lia," she said. "I didn't think anyone was going to come. I thought—"

She broke off and shivered. Her teeth were chattering. I glanced at Gabe and Juniper.

"Let's get her home," I said.

Juniper carried her because she was too tired to make the entire trek. Village life had softened her, and prison had leeched her final bit of strength. She laid her head against his shoulder and shut her eyes. I went ahead, and Gabe brought up the rear. We were a grim group despite our victory. Something ominous hung in the air and tinged every breath I took, something that tasted like uncertainty and pain. We were bringing my sister back with us at last, and she would be safe in an ironic sense of the word in that she was now safe to freeze or starve or be kidnapped by people who wanted her blood. And where did that leave us now in regards to the overthrow of the Farthers in the town? Jullia was our only contact with the Blackcoats, and Raine's grip was tightening every day around the necks of those who remained in Iceliss and under his control.

And on top of it all, we were still no closer to rescuing Adam and Ann.

An hour slipped past as we climbed over rocks and fallen trees and crossed frozen streams. Ice glittered around us, slick and black in the darkness. The trees were all straight and foreboding as sentries, keeping watch over our furtive movements. I scanned the blackness for any glitter of red eyes, any hiss of hot breath, but nothing stalked us this night.

Finally, we spotted the curve of the mansion ruins rising from the field of snow blossoms ahead. Everything was gray and faded in the moonlight.

Ivy stirred against Juniper. She opened her eyes and looked around. "Where...where are we? This isn't Echlos."

"We've moved," I said, my voice so gentle it surprised me. "This is our new home now. It's safer for the others. The Watchers won't come here with all the snow blossoms, and it's far from Iceliss and any soldier patrols."

A muscle in her face twitched at the mention of Watchers, and I remembered her strange connection with one of them. I scowled.

"Let's keep going. Jonn and Everiss will be frantic by now."

When we reached the doorway that led inside, I finally found myself able to breathe normally. We'd made it. We'd rescued her and brought her home unscathed. A shiver ran through my limbs at the thought of what could have transpired, and a rush of images filled my imagination—the glint of guns in the moonlight, the crack of a voice yelling for us to stop, the color of blood on the snow. I scrubbed both hands over my face to banish such thoughts.

We were safe now.

Juniper headed straight for the cellar, still cradling Ivy in his arms. I paused in the ruined foyer as emotion prickled my eyes. I took a few breaths to compose myself, and Gabe lingered at my side, waiting.

"Are you still angry with me?" he asked.

I sighed. "No, I suppose not. You did what you ought to have done. I can't fault you for that."

"But you did."

"Well..." It was mysterious to me how easily I was wounded by his actions. "Consider it forgotten."

He smiled in relief. "And the rescue went perfectly," he said.

"Yes," a voice said behind us. "It did."

Gabe and I whirled. I gasped aloud.

Standing in the shadows, his long dark hair hiding half his face, was Korr.

SIXTEEN

A SHIVER WENT through my whole body like a static spark. Everything was silent and roaring at the same time. I fumbled at my belt for my knife even as my mind spun with horror. We'd been discovered at least. I yanked out my pitiful defense and brandished it at him.

"Boo," Korr said, smirking at us both as he stepped from the shadows and into the pale moonlight coming through the holes in the ceiling.

Gabe started forward, his face contorted in anger, his arm raised. "How dare you—"

The nobleman caught his brother's arms and yanked him around into a headlock, laughing. "Easy, Gabriel. You never were able to best me in a fight when we were younger, and you certainly won't now. You'll only hurt yourself."

Gabe struggled against his brother's hold. "What are you doing here? How did you...?"

"It's good to see you too, brother. How did I find you? It was as easy as setting a trap and laying out the bait. I noticed Ivy Weaver was making a lot of trips into the wilderness, so I arranged for her arrest and subsequent deportation...and then I arranged for her rescue. I thought someone might bite. And I was right."

Gabe and I both went still as his words sunk in.

Korr chuckled. "And you did everything exactly as I hoped you would, right down to replacing the prison key after you used it."

I shuddered at the realization that he'd been watching us the whole time.

"What do you want with us?" Gabe managed. "Are you planning to turn us over to Raine?"

"No. I wanted to see who was planning this little revolution."

How did he know about that? My eyes widened. Korr grinned.

"Oh yes...I have ears everywhere. I caught wind of your plans, and I had a suspicion that Lia Weaver might be involved. But I didn't realize you two were so cozy." He paused. "I've been looking for you, brother. I feared you were dead."

Gabe made a sound of derision that turned into a choke as Korr tightened his arm.

"Let him go," I snapped.

He looked at me over Gabe's head and dimpled. "You're downright defiant in the face of peril. I've always liked that about you, Lia Weaver. It's a quality you share with Ann Mayor."

Ann. I felt the blood drain from my face.

"Shut up, Korr," Gabe gritted between clenched teeth.

"With that attitude, you'll never get my help."

Help. That single word, dropped as carelessly as a stone into a pond, sent ripples of astonishment through me.

"Your help?" I demanded. What sadistic joke was this?

Korr *tsked.* "You do have a glaring character weakness, Lia Weaver. You write people off too quickly. You've never stopped to consider, for instance, that I might want all the same things that you do."

He was toying with us. I wouldn't fall for it. "You want the liberation of the Frost?"

154

He laughed. "Well. Not quite."

I waited for him to elaborate on his lies.

"Oh, I see that doubt in your eyes." He released Gabe and gave him a shove between the shoulder blades, sending him stumbling toward me. "Korr the monster couldn't possibly want anything but the blood of children to feed upon." He waved a gloved hand. "Do you really think I have the slightest shred of loyalty for the Aeralian dictator?"

Gabe reached my side and grabbed my hand. He and I exchanged a glance.

"Well," Korr said, taking obvious note of our handclasp but not commenting on it. "I don't. I'd like to see him overthrown, and I belong to a group of loyalists called Restorationists who want the same." His eyes crawled up to our faces again, and he scrutinized mine so thoroughly that I felt as if his gaze might strip the flesh from my bones.

"You won't get the crown," Gabe said hoarsely. "You aren't in line for it."

Korr fixed him with a withering glare. "If you think for a second that I want that, then you've never known me, brother."

Gabe didn't respond. His fingers squeezed mine so tightly I winced.

"So, do we have a deal?" Korr asked me. "Your assistance with a few matters in exchange for mine?"

"What could you possibly propose to help us with?"

"For one thing, you're all starving. You need food and supplies if you're going to survive the rest of the winter."

"We—" Gabe began, and stopped when I shook my head at him.

Korr lifted an eyebrow and looked at me.

I was unwilling to admit anything about the levels of our deprivation to him. He was the enemy. He was fishing for information, trying to assess the extent of our weakness. We couldn't give him anything. Besides, with the greenhouse and the meager stores from the mansion cellar, we had enough. We could scrape by. But I'd rather let him think we had nothing. That way, he'd underestimate us when he and his soldiers tried to chase us down.

Korr shrugged at my silence. "Fine. Perhaps more importantly, I happen to know the whereabouts of a few people you may care about. Ann Mayor...and that revolutionary, Adam Brewer. And I'm willing to exchange that information for certain assistance, as I said."

Ann. Adam.

My stomach flipped. It was as if the floor opened beneath me and the walls crashed down. He was offering the one thing that had seemed impossible until now— the information about our friends. My heart throbbed. I dared not accept this poisoned gift he was offering, but oh, how I wanted to do so.

Korr gazed at me steadily. "You may not trust me now, but you must if you ever want to see them again."

I found my voice. "Another trap? You arrange for their capture and deportation so you have something with which to ensure our compliance, just as you did with my sister?"

His eyes narrowed. "Actually, no. Your precious Adam was apprehended miles from here, on Aeralian soil, caught red-handed in the middle of a mission. I had nothing to do with it. Ann was implicated in the matter, and Raine wanted her taken out and shot as an example to the village and that lapdog of a Mayor. I managed to save her by taking her to Aeralis under my protection, where she remains now. And I can bring her back here in exchange for what I need, although why you'd want her here in this dangerous, desolate land, I don't know."

"Don't pretend you care what happens to her," I snapped. "Of course we want her back. This is her home."

His gaze flickered at my harsh words, and a prickle of something like wonder touched me. Could this heartless creature be harboring some shred of feeling for Ann?

I shoved that thought away for later, when it might be useful to examine it. Right now I was face-to-face with the snake, and I couldn't afford any distracting musings.

"And as to your sister," Korr said, "you're fortunate that I had her captured before Raine got wind of things. He might have ordered her shot too, you know. I merely cooled her heels in a cell for a few hours until you could arrive and take her off my hands. And of course, so you could show me where you were keeping house these days, and I could make you my offer properly."

His offer. His miserable mockery of an offer. I trembled with rage. "And what exactly is it that you want from us?" I asked, making every word sharp as the cut of a knife.

"My girl," he said, as if surprised I even needed to ask. "I need access to the gate at Echlos and the PLD."

Another fist of shock punched me. I struggled to reply in an even tone. "The PLD was lost—"

"I know you got it back," he interrupted. "Don't try to pretend otherwise. Ann told me what happened."

An unidentifiable emotion stabbed me in the gut. It might have been the feeling of everything falling to pieces. "I..."

"Listen to me," Korr said, and for a moment all his usual sly smirking and posturing was replaced by a

157

fierce earnestness that shone from his eyes and laced his voice. "I must have access to both the gate and the PLD in order to overthrow the dictator. I know you have it. You're using it for child's play—shuttling survivors back and forth, playing at exploring, pretending to use it. But you're wasting it. I can free a nation with these devices."

I took a step back. His gaze narrowed, and he seized my wrist. He brought his face close to mine. I was fixated by the gleam of his teeth. They were sharp, wolf-like.

"Don't be a fool, Weaver. Don't refuse the only chance you'll ever have to get your friends back. Trust me, you won't get another."

"I'll never trust you," I hissed.

Korr dropped my wrist and stepped away. "Fine. I will deliver Ann Mayor to you as a gesture of goodwill."

My heart thumped. "Bring her to me unharmed, and then we'll talk about the PLD."

"I will bring her here, to this desolate ruin, so you had better not flee the Frost in the meantime."

I made no promises. I said nothing.

With one last look at us, he turned on his heel and vanished into the darkness with a swirl of his cloak.

Shaken, Gabe and I stood alone, staring at each other. Finally, we shook off our mutual stupor and walked together to the cellar.

"What now?" he asked in a low voice. "You aren't seriously considering making a deal with him, are you?"

"Of course not. I've promised him nothing yet, and I won't. But I'm willing to risk further contact with him if it means even a chance of getting Ann back."

We opened the hidden door and descended the steps to the cellar below, where we found Ivy wrapped in blankets and sitting at Jonn's table. Juniper and Jonn talked quietly over a pile of books, the ones I'd found in the ruins of Borde's study.

My gaze slid over the new place we'd started to make into a home—the dirty stone walls streaked with fresh soot from candles we'd lit, the earthen floor trod with footprints, the cots and bundles of bedding on the ground, the shelves of canned food, Jonn's new table, constructed from pieces of a shelf laid across two large stones from upstairs. It was a grim place, but there was something cozy and warm and safe about it, too. We had food and shelter, and we were safer here from soldiers and cold and Watchers than anywhere else I could imagine. And now we'd have to leave again. Korr knew where we were. Our location had been compromised.

Where would we go now? Back to Echlos? On to a new ruin? We were running out of options. Our back was pressed to an icy, hungry wall.

I needed to tell Jonn immediately so we could make plans. My stomach shriveled at the prospect of breaking the news to him, but I didn't wait. I couldn't. I crossed the room to his table.

"Where've you been?" he demanded when he spotted me. "Ivy and Juniper came down ages ago." His gaze cut to Gabe, and he grinned knowingly. I knew what he was thinking, and it only made what I was about to say worse.

The words stuck in my throat. He looked happy. In his mind everything must be perfect. Ivy was with us. We were safe now. He even seemed to think Gabe and I were patching things up between us.

And I was about to shatter it all.

"There's been a complication."

Jonn's eyebrows drew together sharply. I supposed he'd come to recognize that tone to mean things were about to implode.

"What complication?"

I explained tersely, using as few words as possible as I laid out the information that would ruin everything we'd worked for in finding this place. "Ivy's arrest, our easy rescue of her—it was all a trap," I finished. "He wanted to find us, and now he's going to return with soldiers and arrest us all if we don't flee."

Jonn sat unmoving for a few minutes, staring at a spot on the ground. When I tried to speak, he held up a hand for quiet. His lips moved a little, but nothing he said was audible to me. Finally, he raised his head and tapped a finger against the table.

"Why not bring the soldiers with him now?"

"I...what?"

Jonn leaned forward. His eyes burned bright as they met mine. "If Korr really wanted to arrest us all, why didn't he bring the soldiers with him when he followed you?"

"Because they'd attract far too much attention," I said. A burst of irritation flared in me. "Don't tell me you think he's telling the truth, Jonn."

"All right, so maybe he doesn't bring the soldiers tonight," Jonn argued. "But he could have. He could have brought three or four with him easily, armed with weapons, ready to arrest us. And if not that, why didn't he simply note the location of our hiding place and return tomorrow with even more soldiers? Why speak to you first? Why give you the chance to get away?"

"Because he's a sadistic man and he likes playing games," I said.

"Or he truly wants a deal, and he's willing to cross the Frost at night alone to make it. He's even offered to help us get Ann and Adam back. He's a cunning man. He doesn't make stupid mistakes, not as simple of mistakes as those. I think maybe he's telling the truth. Maybe he really does want to work with us."

"I don't trust him, Jonn. I won't."

My brother sighed. "Well, we can't go anywhere tonight, not with this number of people and the danger of Watchers." He looked around the room at the sleeping fugitives. "And what about Ann? What if he brings her here, and we're all gone?"

"I'd come back and find her," I said. "I can move quietly alone. I can elude any soldiers he might bring. But the rest of us have to get out of here."

"I think he's telling the truth," Jonn repeated.

"And I think you're insane. This is *Korr* we're talking about. Ask Gabe. He can't be trusted."

"I shall ask Gabe," he said, scowling. "I'm sure he has many insights he can offer us. He grew up with the man, after all. What does he think?"

"He doesn't trust him, of course. And neither should you."

Jonn was clearly resolute, and I didn't have the strength to continue arguing with him that night. I'd run through the Frost twice, sneaked into the village, rescued Ivy, and faced Korr's insanity. Every last drop of me was spent. Exhaustion paved my veins with roads of stone. My eyelids were leading a rebellion against my will to keep them open, and the lids were winning. I stumbled toward an empty cot, sank onto the mattress, and surrendered to unconsciousness.

~

When I woke, I found Everiss bending over me, her forehead wrinkled with what looked like concern.

I jerked upright. "What is it? What's wrong?"

"You slept so late...are you well?"

"I'm fine." I threw back the blanket that had become wadded around my waist and swung my legs over the

161

side of the cot. Every muscle in my body protested as I moved, and my skin hurt in various places where I'd been scratched by branches the night before. My ankle throbbed for some unknown reason. But I had other things to worry about today. I looked around. The cellar was nearly empty.

"Where are the others?"

"Jonn and Gabe needed them upstairs," Everiss said. "To help with the camouflage project."

"Camouflage project?" I repeated. What was she babbling about? "What's going on?"

I didn't wait for her to explain. I grabbed my cloak and climbed the steps to the upper level to see what madness awaited me.

Six of the fugitives were in the kitchen, following orders as Jonn directed them from a chair. Gabe stood at the far end of the room, waving a pair of men forward as they struggled with what appeared to be a section of crumbling wall paneling.

"What's going on?"

"Good morning, sister," Jonn said. His voice was cheerful again. Too cheerful.

My eyes narrowed. "You didn't answer my question."

"You didn't say good morning."

I crossed the room in three strides and braced my arms on either side of his chair. I wasn't playing silly games, not when we had no time, and he knew it. "What are you doing, Jonn?"

He dropped the smile. "We decided we can't move again, not with the food sources and the greenhouse here."

"*We've* decided? Who is this *we*?"

"Me. Gabe. Juniper. The other fugitives."

"You went over my head! You decided without me."

162

"You were sleeping," he said.

"So we just sit here, waiting to be arrested?"

"No. We've decided to take the route of subterfuge instead."

"Subterfuge?"

"Yes." He waved a hand at the wall they were bringing in. "We'll disguise the entrance to the cellar— it's hard to see anyway—and then we'll create a false location elsewhere in the house where it would appear that we had been living, but fled. If Korr brings any soldiers, he'll simply think we ran away."

Everyone gazed at me hopefully. I was their unofficial leader, and they knew things would go smoothest if I agreed.

I crossed my arms and chewed my lip. It was a good plan, and I wasn't afraid to say so, even if my brother did get a little smirkish at my admission of such. "This might work."

"Might?" Jonn protested. "It's a solid—I daresay brilliant—plan."

"Might," I repeated firmly. "And where's Ivy?"

"She's upstairs, helping create the false settlement rooms."

I headed for the hall, following the faint murmur of voices. At the top of one of the staircases, another group of fugitives pulled bits of debris into heaps and arranged small stones to make fire pits. Ivy stood by the far wall, fiddling with the broken furniture.

"We'll burn the debris to make it look as if we've been having fires here," she was telling another fugitive. "We can stuff up these windows to make it less exposed to the elements..." She spotted me. "Lia, come see what we're doing."

"Are you sure you should be up right now?" I put my hands on my hips and surveyed the scene. It did look

163

rather convincingly like the sort of hovel a group of ragtag refugees would use as a hiding place, if the people looking were unaware of the cellar.

"I feel fine," she said. "I spent several hours in a cold prison cell, resting. They fed me water and gruel. Then I had an invigorating hike through the wilderness and a refreshing sleep."

"If by 'invigorating hike' you mean you were carried in a near-coma by Juniper..."

"I'm fine," she repeated, and I let it drop. Because truthfully, we needed her help, and weak or tired was far better than arrested or dead.

I left them to finish perfecting the touches on our fake camp and I returned downstairs to see how the camouflaging of the cellar was going.

The others had fixed the ruined piece of paneling across the middle of the pantry, making it appear to be the back wall. The paneling was secured in such a way that it could only be moved from behind, meaning they'd never find a way to open it without breaking down the wall. It also meant that we'd always have to have someone in the cellar to let us in unless we too wanted to break down the wall.

"Well?" Jonn asked, after I'd surveyed the work.

"It really is impressive," I admitted. "But I don't like this. I don't like sitting here like rabbits waiting for Korr and his soldiers to come and trap us in our own home."

"Of course you don't," Jonn said. "You like doing things, Lia, and you always have."

"Doing things?"

"You like keeping your hands busy with quota. You like running the paths to and from the village. You like reluctantly rescuing Farther fugitives and going on missions and forcing your obstinate little sister to mind and work and keep her feet on the ground and her head out of the clouds. But you're not so good at the sitting and waiting part. That was always my job."

I met his eyes with a sheepish smile. "Then perhaps you can teach me how to do it."

~

I tapped my fingers against the edge of the table as I contemplated my next move. Jonn sat opposite me, composed outwardly, but I could tell by the shine in his eyes that he was excited about his prospects of winning.

Everiss and the fugitive woman named Dara leaned against the table, watching us play. I suspected they were both secretly rooting for Jonn.

"What did you say this game is called?" Dara asked.

"Chess," Jonn said. "I read about it in Meridus Borde's books." He lifted one of the pieces Juniper had whittled out of firewood and set it decisively down in front of my king.

"Check."

I rested one finger on my bishop, trying to concentrate on my next move, but my mind wasn't really on the game. Jonn was going to win no matter what I did, and I couldn't keep my thoughts focused. They ran in every direction like wild horses refusing to be corralled. When would Korr return with Ann as he'd promised? Was he lying, or would he really try to use her to get what he wanted? Would he bring his soldiers? It had been almost three days since we'd altered the appearance of our living space, and we'd heard nothing stirring above. We'd refrained from going out of the cellar during daylight hours, and I was beginning to feel like a buried corpse.

I moved the bishop. Jonn immediately captured it.

"You aren't focusing," he scolded.

"Jonn," I said. "I think I need to be upstairs."

"Right now?" He glanced at the staircase as if he expected soldiers to come bursting down them any moment.

I shook my head, then slowly nodded. "Well, now and indefinitely. At least until Korr comes. We don't have the freedom to pop in and out of here, not without potentially revealing our hiding place, and if he really does come with Ann, then someone has to be there."

"That's a terrible idea. What will you do for food, for shelter? You're just going to live up there alone?"

"Yes," I said. "I think I must. I'm going mad down here, cooped up like an animal in its hole. I need to be with the air and sky and snow. I can sleep in the greenhouse. Someone has to do it...someone has to wait for her arrival."

Jonn chewed the inside of his lip and stared at the chessboard. I knew that he knew he couldn't stop me.

"You'll know it's me if I give three knocks on the paneling with three beats between each." I demonstrated on the table. "Have someone stay at the top to listen, a sentry of sorts. They can let me in if I need it."

"And if the soldiers make you reveal our location at gunpoint?"

"I'd die first," I said, and I meant it.

He sighed. "I don't like this."

"I know. But you're the one with all the practice in waiting, not me." I got up from the table and headed for my bed to gather my things.

~

The air was sharp and cold above ground, and it tasted like snow and freedom. I inhaled deep lungfuls as

I slipped through the interior ruins, listening for voices or footsteps.

Nothing stirred but the sunlight as clouds scudded across the sky.

I picked berries still crusted with ice and ate them even though they numbed my lips and tongue. I perched on the steps of the ruined back porch, a vast marble structure that had once probably been the location of grand galas and parties. It made me think of the village and all the stones that formed the bones of our homes and shops. They had once been the walls and floors and streets for another world. That other world had perished, but they had remained, weathering the cold and wind and ice to cradle another, more primitive people within their stony boundaries.

Would the Frost always be this way—a place where things were hidden, buried, and on the brink of death? Or would the liberation we plotted bring with it something new, something wonderful? Could the Frost become a place of happiness?

Thinking that made me think of Adam.

Hours passed. I didn't have the heart to think of things like love or romance, so I didn't try to imagine what could be in an impossible world. But still, I ached for Adam down to my bones. I wrapped both arms around my middle to hold in the hurt, but it seemed to go on and on, radiating from me like an unbridled fire that threatened to consume me until I was nothing but ashes.

Was this love? Did it always hurt so much?

The faintest skitter of sound met my ears, and I straightened. The hairs on the back of my neck prickled as I slid off the railing and melted into the bushes. Was that a footstep, or just a bird foraging for food on the roof?

There it was again. A whisper of noise. A scrape. A footstep.

Soldiers? I held my breath and didn't move as visions of gray-clothed, grim-eyed figures crept through my head.

Then I heard the voice, hesitant, lost.

"Lia?"

SEVENTEEN

IT WAS ANN'S voice. My heart drummed and my breath caught, but I didn't move, not yet.

It could be a trap.

I heard her footsteps louder now. "Hello? Is anyone here at all?"

She appeared on the porch, clad in a thick gray cloak instead of her familiar red one. I took in every detail. Her hair was longer, fuller. She seemed paler than I remembered, but less emaciated. Wherever she'd been, they'd been feeding her.

Ann's head swiveled in my direction. Her eyes widened as she spotted me among the vegetation.

"Lia?" She took a step toward my hiding place and lowered her voice. "It's all right. No soldiers."

He'd done it. Korr had done it. He'd brought her back. I scrambled forward from the bushes and threw my arms around her. She was solid and warm. This was not a dream.

"I can't believe you're here, you're safe...how did it happen? How did you find us?"

"Well, I didn't come here alone," she said.

"What do you mean?"

Ann nodded toward the doorway behind us. Korr stepped from a shadow and appraised me without speaking. The wind stirred the ends of his hair and made the bottom of his cloak dance.

My stomach twisted.

"Listen to me, Lia," Ann said, and she spoke in a voice too low for Korr to hear. "He isn't what we thought. He isn't what he seems. Please, I know you have no reason to trust him, but you must. He will help us overthrow Raine. He will help us get the Frost back."

"He told you those things?"

"Yes."

"And you believed him?"

"Yes." She put a hand on my arm. "Lia, some things have changed."

I drew back. "What things?"

Ann bit her lip. She hesitated as if considering what to tell me, then she shook her head. "Where are the others?"

"I can't tell you until I'm sure I can trust you."

Hurt shimmered in her eyes. "Lia. It's me."

"Well, I can see it's you, but here you are talking about change and trusting Korr. For all I know, they've brainwashed you in Aeralis."

She sighed. "Can we walk a little? That garden looks...fascinating."

I recognized the invitation to explain for what it was. I nodded. She looked over her shoulder at Korr, giving him a glance I couldn't decipher. He didn't move.

We descended the stairs together. I breathed easier once we were away from Korr's piercing gaze. "What is going on?"

"It's a long story," she said. "But I trust him."

We reached the bottom of the steps and turned right, following a crumbling path.

"When the news first came of Adam's arrest, I was implicated in his crime. Raine immediately ordered my execution. Korr was the one who stepped in to save me. You should have seen him. He was like an angel of destruction. I thought he might physically strike Raine.

He said he needed to take me to Astralux for further questioning, and that the dictator himself might be interested in the whole affair, and Raine's hands were tied. He had to let me go to Astralux to be interrogated." She paused. "Korr saved my life."

"Saved your life? You were taken away to be interrogated. He flung you from the frying pan into a fire he'd built himself!"

"I wasn't interrogated in Aeralis," Ann argued.

"What?"

"Well," she said. "He didn't turn me over to the Aeralian dictator and his interrogators. Instead, I spent almost eight weeks living in his house, unharmed, *protected* I daresay. He asked me a few questions, but that was all. During that time I was contacted by several members of the Thorns, and I managed to complete several missions. Whether or not Korr knows this, I don't know. He has his own agenda, and it is not so contrary to our own. He wants to see the dictator deposed. He wants to see Aeralis returned to the way it was before. And he'll help us if it'll get him what he needs."

I could barely believe it, but Ann's eyes blazed with a fervency that I couldn't refuse to acknowledge. She believed he was trustworthy. She believed he would help us and not betray us. The question now was: could Ann's belief be trusted? Did we need his help if we were to have any hope of recovering the Frost?

I sighed. "I will speak with him. And I will speak with Jonn and Gabe. But I am making no promises."

"I know," she said. "I'm not asking you to blindly follow him. I just want you to allow yourself to consider the possibility of an alliance."

171

I blinked at her, my once timid, fragile friend, now vibrant and strong as she stood before me. "You've changed."

"We've all changed," she replied, and a ghost of a smile brushed her lips. "Even you, Lia. Especially you."

I didn't know if I liked that idea or not, but it didn't matter now. I turned to head back to the porch.

It was time to speak with Korr.

~

Gabe, Jonn, Ann, and I traveled through the forest at dusk, heading for the place where we'd agreed to meet Korr, a clearing halfway between the mansion ruins and the village of Iceliss. Jonn rode the gelding, who we'd been stabling inside one of the mansion rooms nearest the gardens. His sides had grown fat from grazing on shrubbery in the former garden of the Compound director's wife, and he tossed his neck and snorted at the snow with the spunk of a colt. Gabe walked in front, his shoulder set in a rigid line and his chin high. He didn't speak to any of us. Ann and I made up the rear, walking so close that we occasionally bumped into each other.

"He's angry about Korr," she observed, studying Gabe's back. "And I don't blame him. He has had little reason to trust his brother until now."

"None of us did," I reminded her. "We still don't."

"He protected me, and returned me safely to the Frost just as he promised you. And you need his help just as he needs yours."

"We'll see," I said.

She gave me a look that said she was tired of hearing that. I gave her a look that said to get used to it. And we both smiled, because we were friends even though we were not seeing eye to eye, and she was here again, safe, and I was glad.

We reached the clearing and our footsteps slowed. The remnants of a dying sunset were visible beyond the branches, and I saw the first few glimmers of stars. Snow blossoms lined the perimeter of the trees, creating a circle of blue filled with the shocking brightness of snow. In the center of the clearing stood Korr, his cloak a billowing streak of black against the white. He didn't move, but his stillness crackled with energy. His hands dangled at his sides in a way that suggested he was seconds away from reaching for a hidden weapon. He raised his head slowly as we approached.

Jonn dismounted and limped forward on one crutch. Gabe walked beside him, his movements stiff. I hung back to tether the gelding to a limb, and Ann lingered uncertainly a few feet from me. Her eyes were on Korr. He looked at her and then away. A vein in his neck pulsed. She brushed her hands over the bodice of her gown and cleared her throat.

I left the gelding and approached the others. I spoke first.

"You say you want to work with us to overthrow the Farther presence in the Frost?"

"In exchange for access to the PLD and the gate, yes."

"We use these things. We need them. How can we just give them to you?"

"You won't have any need of them if the Farther threat is gone," he said. "So I have every reason to want to help you accomplish that, if it will make you more likely to turn the PLD over to me."

It was a valid point.

"I don't trust you," I said. "But you know that."

"I've brought Ann back to you safely."

173

"Then help us get Adam back, too." It was a desperate gamble—what if he refused? What if I was asking too much too soon? If he wouldn't do it, then our chances of ever seeing Adam again were slim to none. I held my breath, strangling silently in every second that he took to reply.

Korr ran a gloved hand down the edge of his cloak. He took minutes to answer. "I will help you recover the Thorns agent."

"And help us expel Raine from Iceliss."

"Nothing would give me more pleasure," Korr said, looking past me at Ann.

I remembered Ann's story about how Raine had ordered her execution.

"Do these things," I said. "And we will give you the PLD."

I reached out my hand and clasped Korr's cold, gloved fingers in agreement. His grip was like iron. We shook once, and his eyes gazed into mine, searing me to my soul. Then he released me.

As easily as the exchange of a few words in the stillness of a forest, we had a new ally.

But I wasn't sure that we hadn't taken a snake into our arms.

~

"I don't like this," Gabe snarled, pacing from one end of the greenhouse wall to the other. "He can't be trusted."

"Which is why I *don't* trust him," I said for the fourth time.

"You shook hands! You made an agreement."

"If he turns out to be a lying bastard, then I'll have no qualms about breaking my agreement."

"He's going to betray us," Gabe insisted.

I propped my chin in my hand and studied him. "You seem very certain."

Gabe flushed. "I have no political aspirations, if that's what you're implying."

"I wasn't implying anything."

He looked unconvinced. "Anyway, it doesn't matter. Neither Korr nor I will have the crown even if the royal family is reinstated."

"Who would?" I asked.

He sighed. "My cousin, if he's still alive. His name is Bartimus, and he is my father's age."

"And if he is no longer alive?"

"Then...I would be in line to rule."

That surprised me. "But why wouldn't Korr be the first to rule if Bartimus were dead? He is older, is he not?"

Gabe shook his head. "I forget you do not know these things, because you aren't an Aeralian. Korr is not my father's child, and thus he has no claim to the throne even though he is technically a member of the royal family. He is not even a prince, merely a lord. It's why he was not arrested or imprisoned when the dictator came to power."

"Not your father's child? But you look almost identical—"

"My father married my mother when Korr was small. We are half-brothers."

"Oh."

Gabe frowned. "But Korr is a smooth talker, and he has always had many supporters in Astralux. There are those who would rather see him than Bartimus—or me—on the throne. He has more experience politically, certainly, especially now that he stayed and made a place for himself while I ran away. And he was often

175

dissatisfied with his lack of role when we were children. If he is the one who succeeds in overthrowing the dictator..."

He fell silent and stopped pacing long enough to hold my gaze. "You can see why I do not trust his motives, politically speaking. Whatever our personal differences might be, I have no reason to trust him with regard to the crown."

"He said he didn't want it," I pointed out.

"And he could be a lying snake."

"True."

There was another pause.

"You didn't run away," I said. "You were arrested, then you were rescued. You're alive now, that's what matters."

Gabe looked like he might argue, but instead he simply shook his head and started pacing again.

"Are you worried he might try to take the crown from your cousin?"

"I don't know what he's going to do," Gabe said.

"Ann seems to think he's trustworthy."

"Ann is in love with him."

Shock sizzled through me. "What?"

"Don't tell me you haven't seen the way she looks at him."

"I..." Surely this was absurd. It was *Korr.* "I don't know what you're talking about."

"Don't you?" His face softened slightly. "She hides it well, the way you do with Adam."

The way you do with Adam.

"Gabe..."

He smiled sadly. "We won't talk about that now. There's no point, not with everything up in the air and a million different outcomes possible. A Watcher could slice me in half tomorrow. Adam could be dead in that prison. You could eat a bad batch of berries and die in your bed." He laughed, short and harsh. "I won't spend the few hours we know we've got fretting about the future, not when we aren't even sure we have one yet."

It was sensible and uncomplicated. I nodded. "All right."

"But know this, Lia Weaver. I love you."

Emotion glimmered in his eyes. He braced himself after he said it, as if waiting for a blow in response. I lowered my head.

"I love you, too. I've loved you for months. You must know that."

"But is it enough?" He asked the question softly, and it broke my heart.

"It's more complicated than that."

"I...I know."

A throb filled me. I wanted to go to him, to touch him, to cradle him close and say something, anything, to smooth away those lines on his face. The impulse was strong, bewildering. I did love him. It was *Gabe*. He had been the first person to ever awaken the fire of that sort inside me. But once awakened, it had gone on to burn for someone else, and I felt helpless against the conflagration. It hurt like crazy and it made me feel more alive than I'd ever felt before. But it was hurting other people, too. I needed to figure something out, and soon.

~

Ann had completely settled in by the time I made my way back to the cellar. She'd piled all the belongings she'd brought with her—mostly plain, thick woolen cloaks, socks, and dresses—in a sack beneath a cot that she'd pushed next to mine. I found her perched on the

177

edge of the mattress, bent over a book that lay open in her lap.

"How are you adjusting?" I asked, sinking down beside her.

She closed the book and slid it under her pillow before answering. "It's not exactly a palace," she said, glancing around at the gritty stone walls.

"Well, technically it is," I said.

A smile slid across her mouth at my joke. "But...it's safe and warm and it's where my friends are, and that's about all I want at the moment."

I reached out and touched her arm, glad she was with us now but unable to find the words to express it.

She studied me. "I meant it before when I said you'd changed. It's hard to know how, exactly, but you're different. More...open. Not softer, but—" She made a helpless gesture with her hands. "I don't know how to describe it."

I shifted, uncomfortable with her scrutiny. "We've all been through a lot. We've all changed."

"I suppose that's true." She hesitated. "You still don't trust him, do you?"

"Of course not."

"Lia..."

"Ann. I'm not going to trust him until I have a solid reason to do so." I changed the subject. "Have you seen your father since you've been back?"

She lowered her head, but I still caught a glimmer of the worry that flashed in her eyes. "No. Korr tells me he is kept busy at Raine's beck and call just as before. At least he is alive."

Did she know about his involvement with the Blackcoats? The truth hovered on my tongue. I took a breath.

"Ann."

She looked up.

"Your father...I know something about him. Something I don't know that you know, but perhaps you should."

I told her what I'd seen, how he'd revealed his identity to me in order to gain my trust. She was very still, listening to every word as if her life depended on remembering them later.

"I can't believe it," she said when I'd finished.

"It's true. I saw it myself."

She breathed out shakily. "He's not a traitor after all."

"Or at least he's a reformed patriot," I said.

A painfully huge smile broke across her face, and she hugged me tight. I let my mouth soften into a smile as well. At least we had something to be happy about.

~

We had agreed to meet with Korr again the next day to make plans in the clearing, and this time, Gabe and I came alone. I'd thought it best—Jonn was exhausted from the previous day's travel, and Ann...well, I didn't know what was between her and Korr, but I wanted no distractions.

He was waiting for us just as before, standing in the middle of the clearing, still but ready for action.

"You've learned to move quietly in the forest," he said to Gabe as we reached the edge of the trees. "You always were the noisiest when we played those hiding games as children."

Gabe clenched his fingers into fists. I reached out and touched his arm.

"Don't let him needle you. Stay focused. We need him to find Adam and free the Frost."

Gabe nodded and let out a breath.

"Korr," I said.

He turned his attention to me.

"We should probably find a better meeting place than this," I said, glancing around at the trees. "It is hardly a secure location, not to mention the fact that we cannot properly examine maps and other materials with no table to spread them across."

"What do you suggest?" he asked, in a way that indicated he knew I already had an idea in mind. "You do not trust me enough to show me where your people are hiding like rabbits these days, and I do not feel particularly enthusiastic about making the long trek to some forsaken ruin, either."

"No," I said. "Not that." I took a deep breath. I'd rehearsed this several times, trying to get it just right—impassionate, casual, so that he couldn't see how much I wanted it. "I was thinking my family's old farm house."

"Soldiers occupy it now," he said.

"Yes, but surely you could do something about that."

"I see," he said, studying my face.

I didn't breathe as I waited for his response.

"All right," he said finally. "I will get the farmhouse."

"Good." I was light-headed, but I blinked and moved on. "And then there's the matter of Adam Brewer's rescue."

"Yes. I will have to accompany you," he said.

"What?"

"I am Aeralian. You'll need someone who is familiar with Astralux."

"Absolutely not. Gabe is Aeralian."

"Gabriel is a wanted fugitive."

He had a point there.

"Besides, you will need me if you want to get him out of prison."

"We'll discuss it once you've procured my family's farmhouse," I said.

He smiled, knowing he'd won. "Meet me there tomorrow at sunset and we can discuss the details."

He turned on his heel and left.

EIGHTEEN

AT SUNSET THE next day, I arrived alone at my family's farmhouse to meet with Korr. My heart beat fast with nervous anticipation as I came within sight of the yard. It was marred by muddy tracks and garbage and overturned barrels, but it was empty. I crept forward, unwilling to trust just yet. I pressed my back to the wall of the house and peeked in one window.

The interior was dark and silent, the air tinged with dust where an orange ray of sunset came through the glass. The boots by the fire were gone, and the furniture seemed to have been straightened a little. I went to the front door and opened it.

"You're here."

I jumped at the sound of Korr's voice, but I quickly composed myself so he wouldn't see that he'd startled me. I slipped inside and shut the door behind me.

"I'm here, as I said I would be."

It was a challenge. *I fulfilled my end, now you fulfill yours.*

He smirked and indicated a chair at Jonn's old table with one hand. "Shall we sit? I've made tea."

I crossed the floor and sank into the chair across from his. I laid my elbows on the table and watched as he poured steaming water into two cups, then added dried mint leaves to steep. He set one cup in front of me, and I could smell the scent of mint curling up in the steam. It made me think of Stone.

182

"I need you to obtain passes for my people to get inside the village," I said. "In exchange for the PLD."

"Fine," he said.

"And of course, we must have Brewer back safely."

"This is going to be an arduous task," he began. "Are you sure you're up for it?"

I thought of the things I'd experienced in the last few months—chases through the forest, time travel, exploration of ruins, kidnappings, and numerous Watcher encounters.

"I am." I spoke the words firmly.

"Good. We will begin at the Seam, a railroad track that forms the border between Aeralis and the Frost. We'll jump a train there and disembark in the main Astralux train yard. From there, we'll have to travel through the city to the north quarter, where they keep the prisoners."

"Can't you just take a carriage to Astralux?"

"I do not want my presence in the city to be known. I have certain people whom I'm trying to keep in the dark. If I enter secretly, then by all accounts I've had nothing to do with his disappearance. Besides," he said with another one of his smirks, "this way is much more fun."

I was not amused.

"And once we reach the prison?" I asked.

Korr smiled, a cold and calculating expression that made me shiver. "I have a plan."

~

"I don't like it," Jonn said after I'd told him everything. "But I also don't see any other way."

They watched me, all of them—Gabe, Ann, Everiss, Jonn, Ivy—looking at me as if trying to memorize my features. As if trying to remember me. As if I was already dead.

"Korr knows what he's doing," I said, barely able to believe the words coming from my mouth.

Gabe's lips tightened, but he didn't argue with me. He didn't say anything at all.

"I have to go," I said. "I have to get Adam back."

In the end, they had no argument for that.

~

The next morning, Korr and I stood shoulder to shoulder on a plain of ice, facing the Aeralian border. The train tracks stretched past, an ugly laceration stitched across the snow.

I was shivering, but not from the cold.

"Remember," Korr said. "The trains decrease their speed because of the curve. They'll be moving slow enough for us to grab hold and jump on, if we do it right."

I ran my tongue across my teeth and resisted the urge to fidget. Anxiety gnawed at me like a rat in my belly.

"Stay calm and focused, and you'll be fine."

It was the nicest thing he'd ever said to me. I gave him a look, but he was staring down the track.

"Here it comes."

The train throttled toward us, a smoking steel snake with a clanging cry. The ground rumbled beneath our boots. My hands tingled. My throat and lungs were so tight I couldn't get a deep breath. The train rushed past, a blur of black, but it was slowing. The chug matched my heartbeat, and then and then and then—

"Grab hold!" Korr bellowed, and we were running, scrambling, our hands catching on any surface where they could find purchase. Korr hooked his arm around the edge of a boxcar door and hauled himself up. I grabbed on and dangled a moment, my feet hanging as the track blurred below and my stomach seemed to turn itself inside out. The train shuddered and rattled and tried to shake me off. My heartbeat blended with the sound of the wheels.

Then, Korr reached down and yanked me into the car.

I collapsed against the gritty metal and shuddered. We'd done it.

Through the open door, white fields and straggling fences flew past. I caught snatches of the Frost before it fell away as we turned, heading for Astralux to the south. The horizon was just a black smudge that grew larger and longer until it swallowed us, and we were in the Aeralian plains. Now the ground below was wet and muddy, filled with half-cut stalks and the occasional dirt road that curved away into the distance.

"It will be half an hour before we reach Astralux," Korr said. "Get some rest."

He settled himself against the wall at one end of the car, leaving me the other. I made a pillow out of a sack of grain and tried to sleep. Soon the rhythmic rushing of the car had lulled me into a fitful slumber, but I woke every time the train jolted. I watched through half-closed eyes as we passed from the Aeralian plains to a hilly country shrouded in mist. Finally, through the gloom, I saw the city.

Astralux.

Black metal towers pierced the sky above Aeralis's capital, and lights glimmered like fireflies atop poles along the streets and bridges and tops of the buildings. Shapes rose from the mist that cloaked the city—domes, spires, clock towers. Airships filled the sky and dotted

185

the ground with shadows. Everything looked grim and cold and dark, but in a harsh and beautiful way that surprised me. As the train rushed across a bridge and into the city, I caught sight of clouded glass and a burst of verdure. A greenhouse.

I breathed out in astonishment.

"Is it what you were expecting?" Korr asked, a light of interest in his eyes as he studied my reaction to the sights around me.

"Not really." I didn't elaborate.

The train rushed through the city on a track that ran high above the slums. Shadows covered us and whirled away like birds, making masks of light and dark across the planes of Korr's face. I studied him while he gazed at the city, and I wondered. He looked so much like Gabe sometimes, but other times, when he was still and serious and intense, he was something else entirely.

He turned his head and caught me watching, and our eyes held for a moment. I was the first to look away.

The train shuddered as it pulled into the yard, and we began to pass between dozens of other cars surrounded by rows and rows of tracks. The wheels below us clacked and rumbled as the train's speed decreased. I saw a patch of gray sky, rusted walls, a few workers scrambling like rats up and down ladders in the distance. Close by, a whistle screamed.

"Move on my command. Follow me, keep your head low, and don't attract any attention," Korr said.

I shifted into a crouching position beside the door. The train slowed enough that I could see the texture of the gravel below.

"Now," Korr said.

We crossed the tracks at a run, ducking from one stationary car to the next, wriggling between the couplings and then running through cold empty space and scraping past chilled metal again. Rust rubbed onto the shoulder of my cloak. My knuckles scraped something sharp and began to bleed. My chest ached from running so hard and fast, but I didn't stop.

We reached the end of the yard. Korr led me into a tunnel. I bumped against him in the dark, and one of his slender, gloved hands shot out to steer me away. We reached a corner and light blinded me. I blinked.

"This way," Korr said.

We stepped into an alley. Metal walls dripping with moisture stretched up hundreds of feet above our heads where the sky was just a thin gray line. Machinery purred in the distance, low and thrumming. I smelled the mingled odor of garbage and flowers. Gray-white shirts hung drying on a rope strung between the walls.

Korr turned left, and I followed. Shadows streaked overhead as airships passed by. We reached the end of the alley, and he stopped again.

"Stay close to me. The city streets are busy, and I won't look back." He produced a hat from the pocket of his cloak. He pulled it over his face and hair, then plunged forward into the city traffic.

I jogged to keep up. Carriages and steam-powered vehicles rumbled past. I resisted the urge to shrink back from the noise and bustle as I shoved through the crowd after Korr, who had his head down and his face covered by the brim of his hat.

The people around us wore long coats of gray and black and glossy brown fur. Everyone seemed to be wearing gloves. Hats with feathers, flowers, and veils covered haughty faces.

A fine layer of soot lay over everything and soon began to collect on the ends of my fingers and on my hair. I supposed this was the reason why everyone wore gloves, coats, and hats, for it was not very cold.

We reached an intersection. Korr glanced over his shoulder once to see if I was still following before he crossed the street amid a throng of people. When we'd reached the other side, he entered another alley, this one wider and cleaner than the one before. Pathways of wrought iron arched overhead, and I heard the sound of trickling water from a fountain.

Korr stopped at a door and produced a key from his pocket.

"Is this the prison?" I asked, astonished.

He laughed aloud, startled. "No. This is the back door to my home."

He let us in and turned on the gaslight. We appeared to be in a basement of some sort. Boxes and barrels piled high against one wall. Straw covered the stone floor in clumps.

"You can change here," Korr said. "What you're wearing now will only attract undue attention at the prison." He opened one of the barrels and produced a stack of clothing. "Here. These were Ann's while she was here. They should fit you."

I took the clothing and stepped into an alcove beyond the boxes. "Turn around."

Korr made an impatient noise that probably was supposed to convey his decided disinterest in seeing me undress, but he did as I asked. I stripped out of my ragged woolen dress, stockings, and cloak and put on a crisp cotton pair of pantaloons, a blouse, and a strange parted skirt. They didn't quite fit me, because I wasn't as curvy as Ann.

"Done?" Korr asked, looking over his shoulder. He grimaced. "They look ghastly on you, but it'll have to do."

I scowled at him and accepted the coat, gloves, and hat that he shoved my way. I couldn't care less what he thought of my appearance, but he didn't have to be such a complete ass about it. We were allies at the moment, weren't we?

"Come on," he said, and I followed him up a spiral set of stairs.

The rest of the house was a blur of shining tiled floors, potted trees, stained glass ceilings, and a massive clock covering one wall that clanged the hour loudly as we passed. Korr ducked into a study and emerged a few moments later, dressed in full Aeralian fashion—a long coat and a new hat, this one studded with buttons. His gloves were jet-black and the fingers were tipped with metal.

He motioned for me to follow him down a long hall. We reached the foyer and stopped at the front door, an opulent carved thing set with glass. He put his hand on the knob and turned to me.

"Don't say anything at the prison," he said. "I'll need your help once we find Brewer, but let me do all the talking when we first get in. I am there to interrogate him and you are my assistant. Understood?"

"Fine," I said.

He opened the door and we went out.

The front of Korr's house looked out over a wide boulevard. Steam carriages and trolleys rushed past. People in long black coats strolled along wide sidewalks. In the distance, I saw a cluster of towers surrounded by a forest of metal. It reminded me of the new walls around Iceliss.

"What is that?" I asked, nodding at it.

"The palace," Korr said shortly, as if he were loath to say any more on the subject.

Was that where Gabe had once lived? I wondered.

He led me down a flight of steps to a waiting steamcoach. We climbed in and sank onto plush red seats, and Korr gave the order for the driver to go. I braced myself for the lurch, and then we were moving, not as fast as the train, but still faster than I was accustomed to. I peered out the window and saw more mansions of steel and glass slipping past.

Korr sat motionless across from me, a breathing statue clad in silk and velvet. His mouth was pressed in a thin line. His eyes were watchful, black as two river stones.

The city around us gradually grew grittier. We descended through a cloud of mist to a lower level where the sun barely reached, and here our way was lit by the gleam of streetlamps that flickered feebly. I smelled sewage and rot. The chug of machinery was loudest here, and I saw no more glittering glass. Everything was rusted metal or crumbling brick.

Finally, the steamcoach stopped.

I climbed out behind Korr and raised my eyes to view the prison. It was tall and square and built of thick gray brick that looked like gravestones. A sign above the door proclaimed it Prison No. 23.

I wondered just how many prisons they had in this city.

"Hold this, assistant," Korr said, and shoved a metal box at me. I grunted as I took it in my arms; it was heavy.

"What's this?" I asked.

"Never mind that." He strode toward the prison, leaving me to follow.

The door swung open on its own before us, worked by some mechanical means. Two soldiers guarded it. Their eyes stared straight ahead as we passed.

Our boots rang on the metal floor. My hands were clammy, and my stomach twisted. I kept my face neutral and my eyes fixed on the place between Korr's shoulders.

Korr drew himself up to his full height and stalked across the floor of the room. He halted before a window that separated the main room from the jailer's study.

Through the window, I saw a man at a desk, nearly buried by a pile of papers. His ghoulish eyes sunk into pockets of flesh that spoke of sleepless nights and too much weak light.

"Have you got an appointment?" he said without looking up at us.

When Korr spoke, his voice was cold and sharp as a blade dipped in ice water. "No, I haven't. And if you keep me waiting any longer, you'll regret it."

The jailer raised his head and started at the sight of the nobleman in his long black cloak. "I'm sorry, your lordship," he murmured. "We get mostly family members come to plead their relatives' innocence, not many Black Hands, sir—"

"Skip to the end of this obnoxious explanation and direct me to the proper cell," Korr said, murderously calm.

"N-name of the prisoner?"

"Adam Brewer. And hurry, I haven't got all day."

The man consulted a book. "Brewer," he read. "Imprisoned for crimes against Aeralis and against His Eminence. He has no visitation rights."

"Interrogation," Korr corrected.

The man's eyebrows lifted slightly. "Do you have the proper authorization?"

Korr opened his coat and pulled out a paper. He handed it to the clerk, whose eyes widened even further.

"Your-your lordship," he stammered. "I didn't know—"

"I trust you can direct me immediately."

"The guard will take you where you need to go."

One of the guards stirred to life.

We followed the gray-uniformed guard down a hall lined with metal doors. Behind some of them came the echo of muttering and coughing. We stopped at an intersection, and faintly, I heard the sound of weeping. A shiver crawled up my spine. If I was ever apprehended by Officer Raine and sent away, would I end up in a place like this?

Korr seemed utterly calm, but my stomach was flopping like a dying fish and my veins felt filled with ice. Would they suspect anything? If we were found out, what would happen to us? Surely Korr would throw me to the wolves to protect himself.

The guard stopped before a door and inserted a key in the lock. My heart jumped at the click. The door swung open to reveal a narrow room with a single barred window. Metal rings lined the wall, and a string of chains dangled from one, unattached to anything. A chair and cot sat in one corner, and on the cot lay a figure, his hands folded behind his head and his legs propped against the wall.

"Brewer," the guard said flatly.

"I won't tell you anything," Adam said without looking at us, in a tone that bordered on weary annoyance.

The sound of his voice filled me with something wild and fierce. I bit my lip to keep from making a sound as a rush of warmth surged through my chest and overflowed into my limbs. He was alive and well enough to speak. He was unbroken in both body and will. I wanted to weep, as ridiculous as the notion was.

"We'll see about that," Korr said.

Adam sat up and turned to look at who had addressed him. His hair was longer, and the ends curled around his ears and over his forehead. Scruff covered his jaw. He didn't look at me or the guard, only Korr.

Korr raised the brim of his hat, revealing his face. Adam stiffened.

"Perhaps I'm not who you were expecting," Korr said, and smiled with half his mouth.

"No," Adam replied calmly. "You're not."

Korr snapped his fingers at me, and I stepped forward. He flicked a finger against the latch on the lid of the box he'd given me, and it opened. A spread of gleaming surgical instruments lay inside. My stomach dropped.

Where had he gotten those? And what was he going to do with them?

Korr selected one, a slender knife with a narrow, almost needle-like blade. He held it to the light as if to inspect it, and the point shimmered. He gave the guard a nod, and the man went out into the hall and shut the door behind him.

"Put those over there," Korr said to me, and I set the box down on the chair.

Adam still hadn't looked at me. He kept his gaze focused on Korr and that knife. His shoulders were tense, but he sat on the bed with the ease of someone entertaining an old friend. He tipped his head to one side and looked from the blade to Korr's face.

"Are you here to oversee my interrogations personally now?" he asked with a bitter smile. "A phantom from my past, sent to conjure up my confession? Did they think that would work? I'll tell you nothing, just as I told the rest of them nothing."

Korr only smiled.

I couldn't contain myself any longer. "Adam," I said, pulling off my hat to reveal my identity. "It's me."

Adam stilled. He stared at me for one long, breathless moment, his expression flicking between astonishment and wonder before he rose from the cot and pulled me into his arms.

"Lia." His breath was a whisper on my neck, sending shivers across my skin. "Is this a dream? I—"

"It's no dream."

Before he could say anything else, I put my hands on either side of his face and kissed him. Adam made a soft sound in his throat and wrapped his arms around me. I felt the rapid beat of his heart against mine, and one of his hands brushed the back of my neck as his fingers curled in my hair. When we parted, his eyes were soft and dark. He opened his mouth to speak.

"Charming, you two, but we have other matters more pressing than your little romance," Korr drawled, cutting him off.

Adam's hands slipped from me as he glanced from me to Korr. His face transformed as he tucked away his emotions. His gaze sharpened. He was all business now. "Tell me."

"We've come under the guise of interrogating you," I explained. "But we're going to get you out of here."

Adam raised both eyebrows. "What does he have to do with it?" he asked me, nodding at Korr.

"He's helping us, as improbable as it might sound."

"Us?"

"Helping the Thorns. Helping me rescue you."

Adam's eyebrows drew together, and he scowled. "I don't trust you," he said to Korr. "Just so you know that."

"Oh, I don't doubt it," the other man said. "But you must do as I say if you want to escape. Now, I want you to hit me in the face as hard as you can."

NINETEEN

THE GUARD RUSHED in at the sound of my shout. He looked at the blood running down Korr's face and raised his gun.

"You idiots," Korr snarled at him. "Inform the jailer. This man is an important Thorns operative. He must be removed to a more secure facility at once."

The guard rushed out.

The jailer stumbled inside the cell moments later, breathing hard. He looked from Adam, who was braced against the wall glaring at us all defiantly, to Korr, who stood with a handkerchief pressed to his face. "What—?"

"This prisoner is a high-level terrorist agent who's been wanted for some time. I want him moved to the palace prison for questioning. In fact, I'll see to it myself."

"But—"

"Arrange it," Korr snarled. "At once, man."

The jailer visibly quivered at the thunder in the lord's voice. He mumbled something and left the room.

"You won't get away with this, dog," Korr said to Adam, his voice laced with venom.

"I'll see you dead," Adam responded fervently, the trace of a smile on his lips. He didn't look at me, but I felt his attention on me just the same. I stood in the corner, saying nothing, as Korr ranted and made threats about the funding for the prison and the capabilities of the jailer and his guards.

More soldiers came. They restrained Adam's hands with cuffs and escorted him out with a guard of four men. I watched, my heart beating wildly, as he was put into an armored steamcoach. Two of the soldiers followed him inside. The other two returned to the prison. Korr stood beside me, dispassionate and grim.

"Nasty little cur," he said to the jailer as he signed a document. "He deserves whatever he gets for striking me."

The left side of Korr's face was already turning purple, and although the cut above his eye had stopped bleeding, it was still puffy and red. Adam had done a convincing job of hitting him, and he'd rather enjoyed it too, I imagined.

"Have them follow us," Korr ordered the driver of the prison vehicle. He signaled to me with one gloved hand, and we climbed into his steamcoach. I sank against the seat and pressed my face against the chilled glass of the window. Korr watched me, saying nothing. He had a tight, satisfied smile on his face as we began to move.

"It's rather like romancing a countess," he murmured, his voice a purr. "Never allow them to think you don't know exactly what you're doing."

I felt sorry for any countesses Korr might be acquainted with, now or in the future.

The steamcoach sped through the city. I resisted the urge to turn and look at the armored car behind us. I knotted my fingers together in my lap as we crossed a bridge of steel and drove under an arch of iron and stone.

Korr directed the driver to turn onto a side road and stop. As our steamcoach slowed, so did the armored car behind us. Korr produced a bottle and handkerchief from his pocket and wet the handkerchief with a few drops from the bottle. He handed it to me.

"Don't inhale this, or you'll be useless for the rest of the day." He gave me a look, then threw open the door and got out.

"It's my assistant," he said, as one of the guards disembarked from the armored car to see what the matter was. "The excitement has been too much for her, I'm afraid. Give me a hand, will you? I'm wearing my best gloves and I wouldn't want to dirty them."

Inside the coach, I rolled my eyes.

The guard approached the steamcoach and peered inside. I had stretched myself across the seat as if I'd fainted. He climbed in.

"Miss?"

I coughed and shifted. "Come closer."

He bent over me, and I thrust the drug-soaked handkerchief in his face. He barely had time to struggle before he went down. I climbed over him and out of the steamcoach. Korr had already done the same with the other guard, and he was calmly holding a gun on the driver of the car.

"Open it," he ordered, and the man did so with a bewildered expression. Korr took the keys from his hand and pressed the handkerchief over his nose and mouth while I helped Adam from the back and unlocked his restraints. The driver jerked a moment in Korr's arms, then sagged forward, unconscious like the rest. Korr hauled him up and put him in the back of the armored car.

"A little help, man?" he said to Adam. "There's another in the steamcoach and we can't very well take him with us."

Adam hurried to the steamcoach. He hoisted the guard over his shoulder and dumped him in the back of the armored car with the others. Korr shut the door and locked it.

"They should be asleep for a few hours," he said.

I peered through the bars at them. They lay in a tangle of limbs, their faces slack and their eyes half-open. They looked dead, but I knew they weren't.

"Now," Korr said to Adam and me, "we need to get out of here at once. I'm not even in the city, according to the official story. We can't risk too many people seeing us, and they'll come looking for these ones after too long."

"Didn't you use your name and papers at the prison?" I asked.

A ghost of a smile chased across Korr's face, but he didn't reply. He just turned on his heel and headed back for the steamcoach, leaving us to follow.

~

We took the steamcoach back to Korr's house and changed into our old clothes. Korr found a cloak and set of plain black garments for Adam to wear instead of his prison uniform. When Adam pulled his shirt off, revealing a muscled chest, I lifted my eyebrows in surprise and then blushed.

"Did you expect me to be emaciated?" he asked, catching my expression.

"I didn't know what to expect. For all I knew, you were missing a hand or a foot."

"I stayed active in my cell. I exercised, I paced. I'm sure they thought me mad, but it kept me sane." He shrugged into the shirt Korr had given him and did up the buttons. "I look like a Blackcoat," he said, surveying himself.

"Speaking of Blackcoats, things have changed in the Frost."

"Tell me," he said, stepping closer. He reached for me, but his hands stopped an inch from my waist.

"Gabe is back," I said.

Adam nodded. A muscle in his jaw tightened, and he let his hands fall.

I reached for them. "And he and I are friends. We're not...I mean, we haven't..." I faltered, not quite knowing what to say. Instead, I stepped forward and kissed him again. Adam stiffened in surprise and then sighed, his hands finding my back, my hair.

"You keep surprising me with that," he said when we drew apart, and his mouth turned in a rare smile.

"I like surprising you."

"I've thought about you every day," he said. "What I could have done or said differently. We did not part happily. Atticus—"

"Atticus is dead. We lost the farm to the Farthers. We had been living at Echlos, in the lower levels.

He lifted both eyebrows. "Things *have* changed."

"Oh, you don't know the half of it."

~

We returned to the train yard at dusk and waited, staring across a dozen tracks at the train we needed to board. The orange light of the sunset caught the edges of the cars and made them glimmer like gold and copper, strangely beautiful things in the midst of clouds of soot. Shouts echoed across the yard, and in the distance, a whistle blared.

"Just get across without being seen," Korr said to Adam. "Keep low to the ground, run at a crouch if you can. The train will already be in motion, because we can only get on once they've inspected it. We'll get one shot at this—don't botch it."

199

A train thundered past, making the ground beneath our boots shake. The clatter of the wheels made my ears ring. I ground my teeth together and waited for Korr's signal.

"Now," he said, as soon as the train had passed.

We streaked forward across the tracks, slipping under and between stationary cars waiting for their engines to take them away into the countryside or deep into the city. A rusty bit of metal caught my cloak and tore a chunk from the bottom, but I didn't stop.

We reached our train and ran alongside as it picked up speed. Korr vaulted up into the car first, and Adam right behind him. I stumbled but didn't fall. I grabbed the edge of the door and hauled myself inside. When I looked over my shoulder, the train was already flying over the tracks, leaving the yard far behind.

I let out my breath and leaned against the cold metal of the car wall. Adam sank down beside me, and Korr settled against the wall opposite us.

The rhythmic clacking of the train lulled me into a light sleep, and I dreamed of snow in Aeralis and Watchers roaming the alleys. I woke, startled and wide-eyed. Adam slept beside me, and Korr watched us both with the gaze of an eagle. He said nothing.

Finally, when the light had faded completely and the world outside was nothing but black melded with silver where the sky touched the snow, Korr stirred.

"Get ready to jump," he said.

Adam opened his eyes, instantly alert. We said nothing as we moved to the open door of the car. Korr joined us, his cloak fluttering, and we stared out at the snow rushing by at impossible speeds. Fear was a breathless flutter in the pit of my stomach, fear and something else that felt like exhilaration. I filled my lungs with icy air and listened to the sound of the wind roaring outside the car, and felt the force of it on my face. Korr whispered, "four, three, two, one—" and we jumped.

I fell through blackness for one agonizing moment.

With a bone-shaking smack, I hit the snow. Wet filled my eyes and went into my nose and mouth. Numbness shot through my upper body and shoulder. I rolled and lay still, stunned. The sound of the train still thundering past filled my ears, or were they just ringing from the fall?

I coughed and scrambled up. Nothing felt broken. Near me, Korr dusted snow from his cloak. His hair was disheveled and he had a new cut on the side of his face to match the one Adam had given him, but otherwise he appeared unharmed.

"Adam?" I called.

"Are you all right?" he asked quietly, appearing out of the darkness and catching my face in his hands.

"I'm all right. You?"

"Never better." A smile touched his mouth and vanished, but his eyes stayed warm. He lifted his head to look at Korr. "We should get away from the tracks."

Korr nodded. Adam looked down at me before heading toward the tree line, which was just a dark smudge against the sky. I followed them, and together we walked for the Frost. Our boots crunched over the frozen stalks of grass, bowed down and frozen under a layer of powdery snow. I felt tingly and shaky and vitally alive. Adam was back. I'd just jumped from a moving train and survived. We were heading home.

Korr left us at the river where Aeralis ended and the Frost began. He crossed the fallen tree and disappeared into the darkness beyond the bank. Adam and I watched him go.

"I don't trust him," I said to Adam. "I don't care who he helps me rescue; he has his own agenda and we can never forget that."

"We share a mind on this," Adam said, looking at me. His eyes darkened, and he reached out to touch my cheek. The air between us smoldered despite the chill.

"We have much to discuss," I said, my voice raw. "You and I—"

"In due time," Adam said. "Trust me when I say we will. But right now we need to get to shelter. It's late."

I nodded.

We covered ground fast, moving in sync, silent and as one. I'd forgotten what it was like to slip through the trees and rocks in a perfect and full silence that was a conversation in itself, a dance of trust and confidence and unity. Adam caught my eye occasionally, and he didn't smile again, but his eyes gleamed in a way that meant he was happy.

The realization came over me like a warm quilt being draped over my shoulders. I loved him. I'd known it before, but...but it was strong now, certain. I wanted to speak it aloud. My tongue sizzled with the words. But I bit them back, because they were not things to be carelessly tossed into the silence, not the first time they were said. I had to breathe deeply to keep from blurting it. Adam heard the way my breathing changed, and he paused.

"What is it?"

Before I had time to reply, a shudder shook the ground, and a guttural snarl slid through the air.

A Watcher.

"Quick," Adam said, but before we could run, the creature emerged from the trees.

It was a big one, the long neck and haunches encrusted with ice, the eyes glowing scarlet as it swept us with its gaze. My heart thudded and my throat squeezed. I reached for my knife as the creature crouched, preparing to leap.

We had no snow blossoms, no extra accoutrements that the Thorns normally carried to protect themselves. We had only my blood, and I prayed it would be enough as I drew out the knife. What if the Watcher attacked Adam anyway? Terror spiked me at the thought.

But before I could cut my finger, Adam flung himself in front of me. "Stay back, Lia," he gasped, and then he withdrew a knife and sliced his hand.

TWENTY

THE WATCHER SHUDDERED at the scent of Adam's blood. The eyes dimmed, and it drew back from him with a jerk of its neck. The snarl faded to a growl.

Shock rocked me. Adam's blood repelled the Watcher? I didn't understand.

But I didn't have time to think, because the Watcher was turning to me with a deep growl and a hiss of hot breath. The eyes glowed scarlet again. The haunches bunched as it prepared to spring, and the thick neck bristled.

"Lia!" Adam shouted. "Run!"

I ignored his command. My heart pounding, I drew my knife across my thumb and shoved it at the creature's gaping jaws. The blood beaded on my skin. It ran red down my finger and a single drop fell to the snow. The Watcher stopped.

Adam whirled on me. "Lia—" He stopped, staring at my cut finger, his eyes widening and his mouth falling open. We were both still as the beast before us closed its jaws and backed away.

I met Adam's eyes without speaking. My mind was spinning as I looked at his hand and he looked at mine. The Watcher plunged into the trees, leaving us alone. We were both panting. We were both bleeding. We were both speechless.

"You're a Weaver?" I managed to gasp. "We're related?"

"A Weaver?" His eyebrows drew together sharply. "No. I'm not even from the Frost."

"But your blood...it turned away the Watchers."

"Yes," he said, his eyes narrowing. "So did yours. How did you discover the serum?"

"Serum?" What was he talking about? "I went through the gate and met my ancestor. He told me the Weaver's secret. All this time and I never knew..."

"Wait," Adam interrupted. "What secret?"

"Weaver blood turns away the Watchers."

"It does?" Adam's forehead knit with surprise. "I never...well, I knew your father had a secret he'd never told anyone else in the Thorns, but..."

It was strange to see him at a loss for words.

"What serum?" I interrupted. "You're saying we are not related, you are not a Weaver, but your blood turns away the monsters just as mine does. Explain."

He sighed. "You asked once how I moved so freely through the Frost, how I was confident to travel at night. I told you I had my ways. Do you remember?"

"Yes. I remember."

He laughed, low and incredulous. "I had no idea there were other ways to evade the Watchers. I simply found a strange substance in a ruin when I was exploring one day, not long after my family had first come to Iceliss. I was inexplicably drawn to the Frost, but my family worried about me. I found a box with a syringe filled with liquid, and I found papers later explaining that the liquid would repel the beasts in the forest. I was young and stupid, stupid enough to inject myself with an unknown substance based on the ancient scribblings of a possible madman's notebook. But...it worked. The Watchers turned away from me if they smelled my blood. But there was only one syringe, and I did not know if I would be branded a witch in the village...so I kept it a secret from everyone, even my family."

"And was there any more?" I asked. My mind was rushing ahead—what if all Thorns operatives could have such an injection?

Adam shook his head. "Nothing that I ever found."

I nodded. Of course not. We never had that kind of luck, not here.

Adam tore a strip of cloth from his cloak and offered it to me. I accepted it and bound up my bleeding finger as he did the same. "We have whiskey at our camp. We can properly clean these when we get there."

"Good. Let's keep going, then."

We resumed our journey. I led the way. The darkness flowed around us and the trees reached out to scrape my face, but I barely registered it. Adam's blood repelled Watchers, too. This changed, well, everything.

The night was half gone when we finally reached the field that overlooked the mansion. The moonlight glittered on the snow blossoms.

"It's beautiful," Adam observed quietly.

"You should have seen it 500 years ago."

He studied me. "It should have been me, you know. I'm sorry you were thrust into that role. You were not prepared for it."

I laughed, a low and regretful sound. "I was a wretched mess about it. But it's good that I went. I learned some things that I wouldn't have otherwise."

"I want to hear about it," he said. "All of it."

"I'll tell you soon," I promised, and then paused, thinking. Relief filled me. "Now that you're here, you can be our leader again."

"Oh," he said, "I don't know. I think you've done a better job than you realize. Perhaps you should keep the role you've established."

I paused to stare at him.

"I'm serious," he said. "I always saw you taking such a position one day. You've just done so earlier than anyone would have expected. And clearly, you've done a fine job."

I flushed at his praise. "I've had to make a lot of uncomfortable decisions." I explained to him about the Blackcoats, the Wanderers, and Korr. He listened carefully, saying nothing until I was finished.

"And do you think you've made the right decisions?"

"We have to do something, Adam. The people are starving. The village is being held hostage." I thought of Ivy, of Jullia, of Edmond Dyer, even of Leon Blacksmith. Many had died or suffered or been forced into situations that were truly terrible thanks to this occupation. It was time for the madness to end. "And our situation here is not sustainable."

"I agree," he said.

We were quiet as we approached the house. Moving through the sea of flowers was restorative. The scent wafted around us, and the petals brushed our hands and tugged on our cloaks as we waded waist-deep through them.

"I imagine there's no threat of Watchers here," Adam observed aloud. "Good choice for a shelter."

His praise warmed me, but I only shrugged. "It was Gabe's idea to come here in the first place. We were looking for food."

Adam's voice was suddenly casual. "You said before that he stayed after his return?"

"They all did. Well, almost all of them." My chest tightened. I was not looking forward to this upcoming complexity.

Adam, perhaps sensing my reluctance, looked over his shoulder and held my gaze. "I will not make it difficult," he promised. "You will see no territorial behavior from me."

Ivy was the first to spot us when we entered the cellar. She almost knocked Adam over with her hug, and he laughed in startled surprise. Heads swiveled our direction. Jonn looked up from his table, and the grin that split his face could have lit up the entire room.

"Brewer," he said when we reached him. "I'm so glad to see you safe. I'm so relieved." He looked at me. "Well done, Lia."

Ann was dozing on her cot, but she woke at the noise and came hurrying over. "You're safe," she said, giving Adam a pleased smile. She threw her arms around me and squeezed me tight.

"I don't think I breathed until I saw you back safe just now," she whispered in my ear.

I looked around for Gabe, but he was missing.

"He's sleeping in the greenhouse again," Jonn offered. "He saw signs of the intruder again, and now we know it isn't the Wanderers this time, so he's determined to find out who or what it might be."

I nodded. I would speak with him later. Perhaps it was best that he wasn't here now.

"What was Aeralis like?" Ivy demanded as soon as everyone fell silent.

"Ivy," Jonn said. "Give them a moment to rest." But I could see he was just as curious, although he wouldn't ask.

Adam smiled and looked to me to answer.

"Wet," I told her. "Filled with fog and metal and glass. All the people wear long coats and hats and gloves to protect themselves from the rain and soot. And Korr lives in a palace, I can tell you that."

208

An expression I couldn't identify slipped across Ann's face at the mention of Korr. She fiddled with her hands and didn't speak.

"Well, that's no surprise," Ivy said. "He's a lord, isn't he?"

More than that, I thought. But nobody else knew of Gabe's former political position as prince of Aeralis except for me and Ann, perhaps, and that meant they didn't know about Korr's former position, either.

Juniper joined us, and I introduced him to Adam. They shook hands.

"Juniper was the first one to find me after I made the jump," I explained.

"And she was one of the strongest jumpers we've ever had," he said.

Adam looked at me with admiration. "Of course she was. She's one of the strongest people I know."

I snorted, embarrassed by their praise. "I vomited on the floor."

"Well, only once," Juniper said.

After a while, the others drifted away to sleep, leaving Adam and me alone at the table. I told him everything that had transpired since his leaving, including my journey through the gate and things I'd learned there. He listened gravely, asking questions only occasionally. When I finished my account, I fell silent and stared at him, marveling at having him back. The memory of what had happened in the forest swept over me—the Watcher, Adam's blood—and then something tickled at the back of my mind. An idea. I straightened.

"I must show you something. I've just...why didn't I think of it before?"

He waited, perplexed, as I rummaged through Jonn's pile of collected curiosities that he kept beneath the table. Books, parchments, journals, instruments...my hands closed over the box, and I withdrew it triumphantly. I lifted the lid and showed him the syringes.

"Is this what that serum looked like?"

Adam inhaled quietly and reached into the box to lift one syringe out. He turned it over in his hand. The contents inside the glass cylinder shimmered and danced.

"I think it is," he said. "Of course, there would only be one way to be sure."

Face down a Watcher. I shivered. Were we really willing to take the risk to find out?

Jonn woke some time later and dragged himself to his table to pour over plans and mutter to himself. I approached him and explained everything.

"The only way to be sure is to test it," I finished. "I can't, and neither can Adam, since we're already immune. Of course you and Ivy would also be unable to test it. We'd have to use someone else." I looked around the room, wondering who among us might agree to such a risky proposition.

"Absolutely not," Jonn said. "It's too dangerous. And to what end? We already have means of evading the Watchers—and we are safe here. No. I don't think this is a good idea."

"Jonn..."

"No," he repeated. "We already have a thousand other things to worry about, Lia. Why is this so important?"

"In case you forgot, the Watchers are dangerous."

"No. I don't agree to this."

"I wasn't asking for your permission, brother," I gritted out. "Just telling you what I plan to do."

Something glimmered in his eyes—hurt? Or anger? "I thought we were a team. What happened to that?"

"I thought so too, before you went and created a fake camp and a false wall here against my wishes instead of moving us."

"You agreed that was a good idea!"

"Maybe in time you'll agree this is, too." I turned to go.

"Lia," he said. "Stop. Listen to me. We can't get divided like this."

I stopped. My anger simmered and then began to cool. He was right. Of course he was right. I sighed.

"What's happening to us? We used to be so united."

He laughed, low and forced. "Well, look at us. You're the de facto leader of the Thorns here now, and I'm..."

"The de facto leader of everything else." A reluctant smile began to work across my lips. "I miss the farm. I miss the simplicity of it all."

"No, you don't."

I opened my mouth to protest, and then fell silent. Maybe he was right. Maybe I preferred this life of danger and intrigue, as terrifying and difficult as it was.

"Fine. We'll wait to test the serum," I promised.

"Thank you," Jonn said.

I went to my cot and tried to sleep, but my mind churned with thoughts.

~

When morning came, before light had touched the sky, I left the cellar and went to the greenhouse. I paused before going in, gathering my thoughts and emotions. I didn't know what I was going to say to Gabe.

But when the door swished open, all thoughts of Adam and relationships fled from my mind.

A young woman stood in the middle of the greenhouse, her back to me. Her red hair was matted and dirty, and her arms and legs were wrapped in rags. Her long cloak was stained and torn.

I realized only after I'd stood there a second that she was holding a gun, and she had it pointed at Gabe's chest. Then I realized it was *Claire.*

A leaf crunched beneath my foot as I took a step back, and Claire whirled. She pointed the weapon from me to Gabe. "You," she snarled, recognizing me. "Go stand by him so I can see you both."

I did what she said without speaking.

"Claire," Gabe said. "Don't—"

"My name isn't Claire," she interrupted. "That was just my assigned name as one of the fugitives. My real name is Clara."

"Not so different," I said.

"Shut up, Lila." She gave me a withering look, and I did what she said. I exchanged a glance with Gabe, and his eyes begged me to let him do the talking.

"Claire—Clara—please listen to me. We were friends on the other side—"

"Friends!" She laughed, low and bitter. "You were going to abandon me there. She was going to abandon me." She waved the gun in my direction.

"No, I wasn't," he said. "Calm down. We were never going to leave you behind."

"Weren't you?" she said, her voice pitching with a note of panic.

"Claire," I said. "Put the gun down and don't be a fool. If you shoot us now, there's truly no going back."

"Yes," Gabe murmured soothingly. "You made a mistake before, but we can talk about it."

I eyed him. Stealing the PLD had been more than a *mistake.* She'd betrayed us. But I let him talk.

"Is that why you did it?" he asked. "Because you were afraid we were going to leave you?"

"I...no." The gun in her hands wavered. "He promised me..." she stopped.

"Who?" I demanded. "Gordon?"

"Quiet." She glared at me.

"Clara," Gabe said, as gentle as if he were talking to a small child. "Please tell us. What did he promise you?"

Her eyes filled with tears. "He said he had a way to heal my mother. She is sick...she's always been sick, and he said there was no cure in his time for what ailed her. But he said that he could give me a bit of the Sickness and she'd take it and be well again."

"Give your mother the Sickness?" I couldn't help myself. "Are you insane? You'd kill her."

"He said those who recovered were stronger, healed of their ailments..."

"Besides," I snapped, "With the PLD in his hands, how were you even supposed to get back here to help your mother in the first place?"

Claire scowled at me. "I wasn't going to let him *keep* it. I'm not completely stupid. He would give me the cure for my mother and then I would take the PLD back and return it to Jacob."

I wasn't sure if I believed any of this. It was all very convenient. A sick mother, a plan to give it back after all...but Gabe clearly believed her. He nodded, his expression sympathetic. I remembered him saying they had been friends.

"How have you been surviving?" he asked.

She shrugged with one shoulder but didn't lower the gun. "On berries, bark, animals I could steal from traps...whatever I could find until I stumbled across this place. I've been sleeping here most nights."

So she was the one who'd made the trampled-down places we'd seen.

"Where did you get the gun?" I demanded.

213

"I stole it from a soldier's pack while he drank from a stream," she said. "I needed to protect myself. And I tried to shoot a few animals, but I never did get anything."

"You're lucky the Watchers didn't attack you," I said.

She shrugged again.

"Let us go, Clara," Gabe said. "Let us help you."

I bit my tongue to keep from protesting. I didn't trust her.

Her hand wavered a little bit, and she stared into his eyes. Finally, she nodded and lowered the weapon, and Gabe inched forward and took it from her hand with infinite slowness. "Thank you," he said.

She nodded and pressed her lips together.

"What now?" I asked.

"We could use her help," Gabe murmured to me.

I jerked my head toward one corner of the greenhouse. I wanted to talk to him without her listening to our conversation. After a moment's pause, he followed me until we were far enough away to speak freely.

"I don't like this."

"She was frightened and desperate."

"She betrayed us!"

"You heard her yourself," he said. "She never meant to give the PLD away forever."

"That's easy to say now," I argued. "She could say anything, and we have no way to prove otherwise."

"I believe her." His eyes blazed with determination. "I think we should let her join us again. She's been starving. Look at her."

She did look pitiful—ragged clothing, gaunt cheekbones.

"We should ask Jonn about it."

"No," he said. "We need to offer her sanctuary now. Otherwise, she'll run. I know it."

I chewed my lip. Now that Adam was back, he should have a say. I wanted to ask his opinion. But Gabe was right. If we hesitated now, she'd probably go. And I was not totally heartless. She was clearly starving.

"She'll be your responsibility," I said finally.

"I know. We can trust her, Lia."

I wasn't so sure...but I trusted him, at least. He held my eyes for another second before turning away to speak to her.

"Clara?"

She was like a bird poised for flight. Her eyes darted to him and then to the door.

"We want you to stay," he said. "You can help us. We need you, and we'll help you."

Her throat convulsed as she swallowed hard. She looked at me as if searching for signs of rejection. I kept my expression neutral. Finally, she nodded. Her shoulders slipped from their rigid posture.

"All right," she said.

TWENTY-ONE

"AND YOU DON'T trust her?" Adam asked, eyeing Claire from where we sat together over Jonn's table. She was crouched by the shelves, scarfing down the food Gabe had brought her. While we watched, Everiss place a clean set of clothing in a pile by her feet.

"Not for a second," I muttered.

He studied me for a moment, silent, and I could tell he was thinking something that he didn't want to say.

"What is it?"

He sighed. "Are you quite certain that you don't have any...emotional reasons for feeling dislike for her?"

"What?"

"Gabe has been very attentive to her."

Did he mean jealousy? I scowled. "Absolutely not. She stole the PLD and gave it to the enemy. I think that's reason enough for me to be hesitant about admitting her into our confidence."

He nodded and dropped the subject.

"I found the device you use to contact the Trio," I said after another moment.

Adam raised his head, listening.

"I found it by accident. The ground collapsed beneath me as I walked through a clearing."

"Those tunnels are unstable now," he said.

"The Watchers...have you always known the place where they rest?"

His eyes clouded over with a memory. "I found it years ago. They guard that device, you know. Their presence ensures that no one will stumble across it. I had the serum in my blood, so they never attacked me. I didn't count on a Weaver finding it." He gave me a tired smile, and I returned it.

"And what did the Trio say about the liberation of the Frost?" he asked.

"They said to do whatever we could. But currently all plans of liberation are on hold. Raine made a new rule that says anyone going in or out of Iceliss needs a signed pass."

"But you say Korr can arrange this now?"

"Yes."

"We need to contact the Blackcoats and tell them we're ready when they are." He tapped the map that was spread before us. "We'll need to find a clearing we can use to gather wagons in order to portray ourselves convincingly as a traveling caravan, as that is the plan. Do you know the pattern of the soldiers' rotation when they patrol the Frost?"

"We never finished mapping it," I admitted.

"Finish, then," he said. "And we can compensate accordingly. Korr will get us the proper passes, and Jullia Dyer will find us the rest of the costumes we need."

"And the wagons?" I asked. "Where on earth are we supposed to find wagons?"

"Leave that to me," he said. "You figure out those patrol patterns."

~

Cold wind whipped the tendrils of hair that had escaped my braid. I brushed them back and shuffled forward in a crouch, my eyes fixed on the figures moving through the trees a dozen yards away.

A Farther patrol.

Beside me, Everiss chafed her hands together to warm them.

"They're heading toward the river," I said softly, and she made a note of it on our makeshift map with a nub of charcoal.

The figures disappeared from sight, and I motioned for her to follow me as I rose and slipped after them.

I would have asked Adam or Gabe to accompany me, but Adam was busy with Thorns business and Gabe was helping Claire adjust to being among the other fugitives again. Everiss had begged to come, and I wondered if she had something specific that she wanted to say to me. She'd been stumbling over her words all day.

"Lia..." Everiss began.

"Shhh."

"Lia," she said, quieter now. "There is something I—"

I held up my hand for silence and listened for Farther voices. I heard nothing but the distant scream of bluewings and the drip of melting ice falling from the trees. I looked at Everiss.

She bit her lip. Her gaze shifted from me to the trees.

I blew a strand of hair from my eyes. "What is it, Everiss?"

"I...it's about Jonn."

I sighed. I didn't want to hear about how she didn't love him *that* way. "We've had this discussion."

"No," she said. "We haven't. The fact is...well, my feelings have changed. I—I love him."

I paused. "What?"

"I love him," she repeated, firmer this time. Almost as if she'd really heard it for the first time herself.

218

Silence fell between us as I grappled with my astonishment.

Everiss turned pink. "But I don't know if he—I mean, I don't know if you—oh, I don't know. Do you think he would ever feel the same?" she asked, twisting the map in her hands. "I know he thinks he's inadequate because of his leg, but I don't care about that. I don't care one tiny bit, not anymore."

I let out a shaky laugh. "Then I suppose you ought to tell him that."

"Yes, but...will you support it?"

I took in her anxious expression and realized she was asking my permission, of sorts.

"He loves you," I said. "That's really all the answer you need."

"But will you accept me as a sister?"

Our past flashed through my memory—her betrayal, her subsequent loyalty, all the disagreements and frustrations between us. Could I? I saw in my mind's eye the way Jonn looked at her, the way they laughed together. I saw her now, flushed and anxious as she awaited my response.

"Yes," I said, and the words were surprisingly warm as they left my mouth. "Of course."

She blinked, exhaled. "Thank you. That means so much to me."

"Let's keep moving," I said. But as we headed after the patrol, I felt lighter. Beside me, Everiss beamed.

We tracked the patrol to the river, where they turned to head toward the village. Everiss made note of it on our map. I checked the sky.

"It's almost sundown. We should head back."

We retraced our steps in silence, but it was a gentle kind of silence that wrapped me like a blanket. I looked at Everiss from time to time, and there was a light in her eyes that looked like hope. Something bubbled in my chest—happiness?

Darkness was gathering by the time we'd almost reached the ruins. We stopped to catch our breath, and Everiss turned to me.

"I know we haven't always been friends," she said. "But I'd like to be now."

"I'd like that too."

A snarl split the air, and we both whirled.

Watchers.

"Get behind me."

She hesitated, staring at the trees as if in shock.

"Everiss. Get behind me." I yanked the knife from my belt and pressed the tip to my finger as I scanned the trees. Where was it? Did she have time to try to run?

The ground shook as the monster emerged from the trees, teeth gleaming, red eyes glowing. It was massive, with powerful haunches and gaping jaws that expelled steaming breath in our direction. I carved a line down my finger and watched as the blood dripped into my palm. The Watcher shuddered and drew back. Its eyes shifted from me to Everiss.

I realized with a shock that she wasn't wearing any snow blossoms.

"Where are your snow blossoms?" I shouted.

"I—I must have dropped them in the forest." She fumbled at her chest and neck. "Lia—"

The Watcher growled. I threw up my hand to stop him, but it was as if I were invisible. The monster leaped over me, knocking Everiss into the snow. She screamed, but the sound stopped abruptly as the Watcher caught her in its jaws.

It happened so quickly. She fell into the snow, limp as a doll, her face slack and her eyes open and unseeing. The Watcher vanished into the forest, leaving churned snow in its wake. I ran to Everiss and knelt beside her body.

"Wake up," I gasped. "Wake up!"

But she was already turning cold.

~

We buried her in the greenhouse, in the far corner beneath a fruit tree. Jonn spoke to no one. When we returned to the cellar, he hobbled to his table and sat alone, staring at nothing.

"Jonn," I said. I touched his arm to get his attention, and he raised empty eyes to mine. He didn't speak.

"Jonn," I repeated. "Before she..." I didn't say *died*. "In the forest, she told me she loved you. She said she didn't care about your leg. She loved *you*."

His throat convulsed as he swallowed. He turned his head and didn't respond.

Grief hung heavy over me, coating my thoughts, pulling at my limbs, muttering in my mind. My eyes burned and my throat ached with the tears I couldn't shed. I was tired of the deaths of my companions, and I was tired of dying by inches every day, beset by cold and starvation and the slow anxious silence of uncertainty and fear. Resolve hardened in me. We would take back what was ours. We would drive out the soldiers and reclaim the village. I would contact the Blackcoats. I would demand that the plan resume immediately.

I turned to go.

"This is my fault," Jonn said. His voice scraped the silence, barely a whisper.

I stopped, turned. "It isn't your fault."

"I said not to test the serum. If we had..."

"We can't know that. She might have refused to take it. It might not have worked. We don't know, Jonn."

221

He shook his head and refused to say anything else.

~

I went alone to the village. Jullia deserved to hear of her sister's death firsthand, and since I was with Everiss when she died, the telling was mine to bear.

She absorbed the news without speaking, and when I'd finished laying out the barest details before her, I fell silent too. The darkness curled around and between us, and I shivered as a chilly breeze touched my cheeks. I was like ice, splintering.

"She died a hero," Jullia said, low and determined.

"Yes."

"Her death will not be in vain. She died preparing for the liberation of the Frost."

I nodded. My own words choked me. I thought of Jonn and his guilt. I thought of the serum. I thought of everything we had left to accomplish.

"We have a plan," I said. "Tell the Blackcoats—I mean, the People for the Liberation of the Frost. Tell them we have a plan, a way to get around Raine's edict about passes. Tell them the liberation will happen."

TWENTY-TWO

DARKNESS SHADED ME as I crouched in the bushes. Adam was beside me, and I was aware of his warmth even though we did not touch.

Before us, in the clearing, Gabe stood holding Claire's gun. He turned it over in his hands, and I could tell he was frightened even though he hid his emotions well.

We were waiting for a Watcher.

The wind stirred the tree branches around us and brought the scent of pine with it. Gabe shifted. His fingers played nervously with the edge of his cloak. He glanced our direction and then away.

"What if it doesn't work?" I said to Adam in a whisper for what must have been the tenth time. Anxiety danced in my chest, a sickening rhythm of fear and dread.

"Gabe wanted to do this," he reminded me, probably because he was tired of explaining how we'd be there to distract the monster with our own blood while Gabe threw a net of snow blossoms over himself and ran.

I chafed my hands together. In my head, I kept seeing Everiss's lifeless body in the snow. I kept hearing her scream cut short. I raised my eyes to Gabe's, and his gaze burned through me.

That was when we heard the distant rumble of a guttural growl.

"Got one," Adam muttered.

The Watcher burst into the clearing at a run, eyes blazing red and mouth open to reveal a row of glittering incisors. Gabe braced himself. His arm that held the gun trembled.

"No," Adam muttered under his breath. "Don't shoot it. The knife, man."

Slowly, Gabe unclenched his fingers and let the gun fall into the snow. He withdrew a knife from his belt and drew the tip across his finger. Red blossomed against his skin.

The Watcher shuddered to a halt.

Gabe didn't move as the creature turned and vanished into the forest again.

I leaned against the tree next to me and shut my eyes.

We'd found the serum.

~

We threw ourselves into a whirlwind of plotting and planning. Adam and I tracked the movements of the Aerialian soldiers until we'd mapped all the trails they always took. We chose a clearing well away from their patrol circuit that we could use to assemble the wagons and other supplies. I continued to meet Korr at my family's farmhouse, which now stood empty. My heart ached every time I stepped through the door, but if everything went well, it wouldn't be long before Jonn, Ivy, and I could return to it.

Resuming contact with the Blackcoats was trickier. They did not yet know we were partnering with Korr, and I doubted they'd trust him. I had to steal into the village at night to get messages from Jullia. Along with the messages from the Blackcoats addressed to "Bluewing," she gave me scraps of cloth for disguises, and food if she could spare it. She said little, and her eyes were always red. Everiss's death had taken something vital from her, but she worked all the more grimly and doggedly since.

I poured over the notes from the Blackcoats with Jonn, Adam, and Ivy once I'd carried them back to the mansion ruins. We'd agreed on a time—two weeks from now. Jonn threw himself into the liberation effort with determinism shored up by grief.

"Two weeks is not much time," he said as we sat at the table, discussing plans yet again. "We still have to assemble costumes, get the wagons, plan strategy..."

"I think we can do it," Adam said. He looked to me. "Have you spoken to Stone?"

"He agreed to meet me two weeks following my release from their camp. It should be tomorrow," I said. "When he comes, I'll make our offer to him."

"Good. Then let's get to work," he said.

~

I waited for Stone in the greenhouse with the supplies we'd promised to give his people. I settled on a chunk of rock that lay behind a cluster of fruit trees and let myself relax for the first time in days. The rays of sunlight scattered light through the glass, and I watched condensation gather and drip on the edges of leaves. It was so hot I removed my cloak.

The door hissed. I straightened and reached for my knife, but instead of Stone, Gabe parted the vegetation and stepped onto the path.

"Jonn said I'd find you here," he said, his tone cautious. He strode over and dropped down beside me. I scooted over to give him some room to sit.

He settled himself and drummed his hands against his knees. They were small, princely hands, but they'd always fit mine perfectly. A place in my chest throbbed with pain, and I drew in a shaky breath.

"We've had a lot of additions to our group, haven't we?" he said finally. "Ivy, Ann, Clara..."

Adam, I finished for him silently.

He was waiting for me to comment. "We've had some subtractions, too."

He nodded. We were both silent, waiting for the pain to pass.

"It's changed the dynamic," he continued. "It's no longer you and me going on missions anymore, is it? You go off with him, because that's how it was before." He paused. "You're glad he's back."

A statement of fact, not an accusation. Perhaps it was a question, too, but an unspoken one that hid between the things he'd said.

I turned my head to study his expression. He was squinting at the sun through the glass. With my eyes I traced the curve of his cheekbone, the dark slash of his lashes against his skin, the way his hair fell over his forehead, long and untrimmed. He was handsome, and even after months of rough living, he had a refined way of moving, sitting, speaking. Something brimmed in my heart—care, concern...love. I joined him in gazing at the light that glittered through the ceiling instead of speaking.

"You and Claire have been keeping close."

"Clara," he corrected softly.

I shrugged.

"I'm glad she's here," he said. "We were friends in the other time." He turned to me, his expression beseeching. "She's a good person, whatever her mistakes were. I want you to know that."

"Gabe..."

"I know you don't trust her now, but—"

I snorted. "I certainly don't trust her."

"Well shoot me, Lia, is there anyone you do trust?"

Adam. His was the first name that came to mind. I blinked.

Another hiss of the door distracted us. Stone. I stood as he approached, and Gabe warily rose to his feet beside me.

Stone stopped and spread his hands in a show of nonaggression. He wasn't wearing his ghostly white mask this time, only a thick cloak.

"I see you survived your run through the Compound after you escaped our camp," he said to Gabe.

"I did," Gabe responded, crossing his arms.

Stone sized him up in a way that might have come across as a challenge, and I laid a hand on Gabe's arm as he stiffened. We were here for purposes of collaboration, not argument or threats.

"Please," I said quietly.

Gabe muttered something about having business elsewhere, and after a dark glance at Stone, he left us alone.

"Lia Weaver," Stone said. "You have the supplies and information you promised us?"

"Yes. And it turns out that we have more to discuss than you know."

"Oh?"

I took a deep breath. Selling people on ideas was hardly my greatest strength. I wished Ivy or Ann was here to do it instead, but they weren't, and they couldn't. They were strangers to him. I was not.

"We plan to expel the Farthers from the Frost in two weeks' time, and we need your help."

I paused, expecting an objection, but he didn't say anything.

I continued, "If your people join us, we might have a chance."

"Join you?"

"We need manpower. We need numbers to stand and fight with us."

His face hardened a little at the word *fight*. He looked pleased, but I could not be sure. I had not convinced him yet.

"And in return?" he asked. "What do we receive in exchange for this costly gesture?" His gaze strayed to my arm.

"Not my blood," I said. "Something far better."

~

The deal I made with Stone and his people secured us the numbers we needed. But still, other things remained to be accomplished, and the deadline was rapidly approaching. We spent hours at the table—Jonn, Ivy, Ann, Gabe, Adam, and me—discussing, plotting, planning.

"Only a few of us have to convincingly pass as members of a traveling caravan," Jonn reminded me. "The rest will be hiding in the wagons. And the Blackcoats will be waiting in the village to come out and fight with us."

"Fight?" Ann asked from her place at the table. Astonishment colored her voice.

"Of course," Ivy said. "What did you think we were going to do, hold hands and dance?"

"It's not going to be a full-out battle," Jonn said. "But we have to get to Raine somehow, and he'll be heavily guarded. If we can take him captive, then we'll be able to force them to agree to our demands. We'll force them to leave Iceliss."

"I thought..." She shook her head. "I mean, fight with what? Capture him with what? Sticks and stones?"

"We have arrows," Jonn said. "Knives. Some firearms..." He looked at me as if for help reassuring her, and I spread my hands helplessly. I'd been so busy focusing on rescuing people and finding food and securing alliances that I had not put a great deal of thought into *how* we'd be liberating the Frost. That kind of thing was Jonn's department.

"What else do we have, Lia?" Jonn asked.

I glanced around the room. "We have cans and cans of supplies, most of them worthless. We have the books and all the other junk I found in Borde's laboratory. We have cots and rags and a lot of hungry people."

Ann knit her fingers together. Her nails were dirty—something I'd never thought I would see. She'd always been so clean, so proper, so stately. "I've seen the soldiers training in Astralux. We will be no match for them. Look at us. We have less than twenty people total, half of whom are either two old or too young for combat. And how many of the Blackcoats do you think will be prepared to fight? How many Wanderers?"

She was right. I looked at Adam and then at all the people I loved in the room. Did we really think we could be any match for trained soldiers, even with the help of the Wanderers?

Adam caught my eye. "What are you thinking?"

I shook my head because I didn't know yet. My feet itched to pace, but I stayed in my seat and listened to the others bicker about strategy and method. Ann fell silent again. Adam traced the map with his fingers, his forehead knit with thought. And suddenly the walls of the room were too close, and the air too dark and dank, and the candlelight too dim. I shoved back my chair and headed for the stairs.

I heard the soft pad of footsteps behind me, and when I looked, Adam had followed. I stopped to see what he wanted.

"Keep going," he murmured. "I want to clear my head, too. We need a little of the Frost in our lungs, I think."

Together we climbed the stairs and went out through the kitchen to the back porch of the mansion ruin. Shadows painted the world purple, and a milky spread of stars glittered overhead like a crust of freshly fallen snow. The air was crisp against my cheeks and nose, but the edge had gone out of the cold with the coming Thaw. I smelled the scent of snow blossoms on the wind, a faint and reassuring perfume that sent a thousand memories cascading through my mind. I inhaled it deeply, savoring one moment of comfort.

"Ann is right," I said finally. "We don't have the firepower to force them to do what we want, not if we're being realistic."

"Perhaps not if we try to go in and face them head-on," Adam said. "But there might be another way."

"But what?" My mind spun as I gazed across the shadow-riddled landscape. I inhaled another lungful of snow blossom scent and closed my eyes. The wind stirred my hair. In the distance, I heard the crunch of some animal rustling in the underbrush.

And the inkling of inspiration—insane inspiration—began to take shape. My stomach churned, and my heart beat fast as I pondered it. It was crazy. It was absolutely mad.

But it might work.

What had Jonn asked me downstairs?

What else do we have, Lia?

We had more than we realized. Much, much more.

I opened my eyes and turned to Adam. The inkling of a plan was taking root.

Footsteps clattered behind me, and Ivy appeared in the doorway.

"Lia. I have an idea."

"So do I," I said, and smiled.

TWENTY-THREE

WE MOVED THROUGH the forest, traveling as silently as a group of almost twenty people could. We were heading for the clearing where the four wagons waited, covered in canvas. Black cloaks clothed our backs and hid our faces, and we carried packs of supplies—rags and paints that would transform us from skinny fugitives into colorful, mysterious caravan people. My brother rode at the front of the group on the gelding; Adam and I brought up the rear on foot.

The two weeks had passed. Today was the day.

Korr waited for us in the clearing, his arms clasped behind his back. He stepped forward to meet Adam and me while the others approached the wagons to get into costume and take their places.

"All is ready," he said, his eyes flicking over our faces as if to judge our trepidation. "I've done everything you asked."

"Good," Adam said.

"And the PLD?" His voice was smooth as butter, but I detected the impatience beneath.

"You'd better hope we survive this," I muttered. "Because you won't get it until the Farthers have been driven from our midst."

Korr opened his mouth to say something else, but then his gaze slid past me, and his expression shifted from cold to incredulous. "Gabriel," he said. "Are you accompanying these zealots on their mission?"

I turned. Gabe stood behind us, his shoulders back and his chin high as he faced his brother's scorn. He didn't look at me.

"I am," he said. "These 'zealots' have rescued and sheltered me. I owe them this, at least."

Korr pressed his lips together but said nothing. His gaze shifted again, and his eyelashes fluttered to a squint. I followed his eyes.

Ann.

She had donned a long crimson dress supplied by Jullia, and snow blossoms filled her hair. A mask made of rags covered half her face, and a bright color stained her lips red. She looked beautiful and strange and wholly different from her village self.

Korr flicked his cloak away from his boots with one gloved hand, a gesture of frustration. "Well, I hope you do not all die, then."

"Don't be too kind, brother," Gabe said. "You'll ruin your reputation as a heartless monster."

Korr ignored his brother and addressed me. "I cannot be here in the Frost if your plan succeeds, lest enraged and liberated villagers try to have my head on a pike, and of course my part in this cannot be known. But I will return for what was promised me."

I nodded.

With that, he turned on his heel and headed for the path in a swirl of black cloak.

Movement stirred in the trees. The Wanderers. They slipped into the clearing and regarded us without emotion. Ivy moved to greet them, carrying the gray cloaks they would need as disguises. I saw Stone among them, and he nodded at me.

Adam touched my arm. "I'll see that everyone is settled."

He left me alone with Gabe. I stood still for a moment, gazing at the way the snow had begun to melt across the tops of my boots, listening to the activity around us and the silence that hovered between us. Finally, I raised my eyes to his.

"We might die today," he said.

"Yes." My voice was so quiet barely punctured the silence.

"Are you worried?" he asked.

And then he was pulling me into a fierce embrace before I could answer, squeezing me tight, pressing his face into my hair. I returned the hug, as if clinging to him for a moment could send strength into me that I desperately needed.

We drew apart slowly, and I let him go. He went to join the others without saying anything else.

Adam found me again. He looked from my face to Gabe's back. His expression betrayed none of his thoughts. "Are you all right?"

"Yes."

"In case we don't survive this," he said quietly. "I want you to have no questions about how I felt."

"Adam..."

He stepped forward and kissed me. I shut my eyes and leaned into him. He slid his hands down my arms to cup my wrists. I couldn't breathe. I couldn't cry. I was frozen in a moment with him, and it was bliss.

A shout sounded. It was time.

We drew apart. Adam touched my cheek once and then he was gone, heading for his post.

I put on my mask and took my place in the first wagon with the others who dared not be recognized by the soldiers. Those whose features would be unfamiliar to the villagers and soldiers took their places around the caravan on foot. The other three wagons carried no passengers.

My heart was a drumbeat against my ribs as the caravan began to move. The supplies at my feet jostled, and the contents of one of the boxes clinked. I put out my hand to steady it, and then I leaned my head back against the seat behind me and stared at the quivering fabric that covered the top, creating a small room around us. Gabe sat with his back to the wagon's side, his eyes closed. Beside me, Ann stirred.

"Are you all right?"

I reached out and found her hand. Her fingers were as cold as my heart felt. I squeezed, and she squeezed back. When I looked at her, her eyes held all the things I couldn't say. Love, fear, sadness. The only thing I didn't see in her eyes was regret.

"You care for him, don't you?" I asked. There was no need to clarify who *he* was. I saw in my mind's eye Korr's proud expression, the sly smile, the flashing eyes. He was sharp and cold and wolfish. His mouth spat sarcasm and sharp wit, and his words leaked with lies. How could she feel something for him?

The corner of her lip curved up in a bemused grimace. She didn't respond, but I knew the feeling well, the one where all the words scuttled away from your tongue, leaving you empty-handed and love-bruised in the wake of everything you hadn't expressed. I slid across the bench and nestled my head in the crook of her shoulder, and she reached up to touch my cheek. We stayed that way all the way to Iceliss, sending strength to each other through the points where our skin touched.

The wagons stopped when we reached the Cages before Iceliss. I strained to hear the crunch of soldiers' boots in the snow, the low snap of voices in the sudden silence as they demanded passes, the rasp of paper being drawn from a pocket. Juniper was our spokesman because they would not recognize him, and I listened to the comforting rumble of his voice as he answered their questions. He sounded calm.

My blood drummed in my veins, hot and frantic. The seconds scraped past.

"Go on, then," the soldier barked.

Beside me, Ann dipped her head low and closed her eyes. Her shoulders rose and fell with a shuddering breath.

The wagons rumbled forward, and in my mind's eye I saw the gate passing over us, the cobblestone streets receiving us. We turned left, past the Quota Yard toward the front of the Assembly Hall. We would set our caravan camp at the back of the square, near the wall.

It would not be long now.

As soon as the wagons stopped, we burst into action. Ann slipped from the wagon and threw a ragged brown cloak around her shoulders. She pulled the hood over her face so only her mask was visible, and then she turned to me and squeezed my hands.

"For luck," she said, and then she was gone, running for her father's house.

I dragged in a breath and released it. I donned a gray cloak. My mask was simple, just a gray strip of cloth, but across the side Ann had embroidered a bird in colors of sapphire and silver.

A bluewing.

Adam found me. He wore a black cloak and a caravan mask with gold and blue stripes. Through the holes in the mask, his eyes blazed with fierce determination. "Raine will address the people on the steps of the Assembly Hall in half an hour."

I nodded, and we parted.

There was much to do.

~

A crowd gathered before the Assembly Hall when the Farther clock clanged twelve times. I slipped among the sea of gray and blue cloaks, carrying a tray of ribbons and baubles as part of my caravan disguise. My heart pounded, and sweat prickled against the back of my neck and across my palms.

Across the square, I spotted the wagons. Adam stood in front of them, juggling a trio of colored balls. A few people clapped politely when he caught all three balls with one hand and bowed.

I reached the steps of the Assembly Hall and turned, scanning the people's faces, looking for Ann. I needed to make sure she was here. I counted the soldiers on the wall that was visible beyond the square. I saw at least six, all carrying guns. My stomach did a somersault. I looked behind me at the Assembly Hall. The Mayor had quietly slipped up the steps on one side and stood at the top, waiting.

There was a shout for order, and the crowd churned and parted as Raine entered the vicinity, flanked by a company of soldiers. Ann stepped into my line of vision at the end of the path that had parted for Raine. She nodded at me.

I drew in a breath. Everything was ready, then.

Raine reached the steps to the Assembly Hall. I blocked his path with the tray of ribbons.

"Buy a ribbon, sir?"

He scowled. "Get out of my way before I have you flogged."

One of the soldiers shoved me aside with his gun, and I fell, scattering ribbons everywhere. I shrieked loudly, and gazes flew to me—the townspeople, the soldiers on the wall, the soldiers surrounding Raine. Everyone was looking at me. No one was looking at the Mayor.

That was the moment that he drew the gun and aimed it at the officer's head.

"Raine," he said, speaking clearly enough that his voice rang through the square. "You've been here long enough. It's time for you to take your soldiers and go."

Raine stopped. His gaze crawled to the Mayor's gun, and then to his face. His lip curled.

"Disarm this blubbering idiot."

The soldiers raised their weapons and started forward.

"Don't come any closer. I'll shoot him," the Mayor said. His arm didn't waver.

"Lower your weapon, fool," Raine said. "You cannot win. You are outnumbered. If you shoot me, my men will slaughter your whole village, including you. You have no means to fight back against us."

The Mayor smiled. "That is where you are wrong."

The sound began as a rustling that grew and grew until it was a crash of snapping wood and ripping canvas. I heard a frightened shout, and the crack of a gun. And that was when the Watcher leaped from one of our wagons.

TWENTY-FOUR

RAINE FROZE, HIS mouth falling open in terror. The soldiers around him swung their weapons from the Mayor to the monster. The villagers in the square didn't move. A few of them trembled visibly, but they lifted their chins and held their ground.

My lips curved into a smile, because we had a secret.

Every person in the crowd below was one of ours.

The Watcher leaped onto the wall and swatted at the soldier who had fired the gun as if he were an insect. The soldier screamed as he fell, and the Watcher snarled and prowled forward, the powerful neck swiveling, the eyes glowing in the sunlight. Another soldier fired his gun, and the bullet sparked off the Watcher's shoulder. The monster didn't even flinch.

"Fools," Raine hissed to the Mayor. "What have you done? It will kill us all!"

"Wrong," the Mayor said. "The Watcher won't hurt any of the villagers here. It won't hurt any of the Frost dwellers. You and your soldiers, on the other hand..."

He didn't mention the serum, because we didn't want the Farthers to know about its existence. He didn't tell Raine that we'd injected every person present with Watcher-repelling serum this morning. He didn't mention that half the crowd gathered before the Assembly Hall were Aeralian fugitives, Thorns operatives, and Stone's people in disguise, and the other half were Blackcoats. He didn't mention that the rest of the villagers were hidden safely away in their houses.

"That can't be true," Raine snapped. "Your people have been killed by them before."

The Watcher reached a second soldier on the wall and opened its jaws. The eyes glowed red. The soldier scrambled away, abandoning his gun, and the Watcher leaped after him with a snarl.

"Shoot it!" Raine bellowed, but the soldiers were paralyzed with fear.

"Lay down your weapons," the Mayor said, "or the monsters will attack you."

Another splintering sound filled the air, and a second Watcher emerged from one of the wagons. This one was larger than the first. It opened its maw and released a guttural snarl. The remaining soldiers on the wall fled as a third Watcher burst from the final wagon with a rip of fabric and a crunch of wood, leaping forward with a bound of its powerful haunches. A red streak glittered down its side. Ivy's Watcher.

"I thought these beasts only came out at night!"

"It turns out," the Mayor said calmly, "that the Watchers have many secrets that were previously unknown. They can come out during the daylight if summoned."

"Who did this?" Raine demanded.

"Bluewing," the Mayor said, and that was my cue.

"Surprise." I stepped onto the stairs and flashed Raine a thin smile. The Farther officer saw the bird emblazoned on my mask and jerked with surprise and recognition. His face turned a mottled red.

"Bluewing," he breathed.

"You've heard of me?"

"I'll see you dead."

"Unlikely," I said, looking behind me at the Watchers.

The third and largest Watcher was heading for the Assembly Hall. As it approached, eyes glowing, the villagers raised their fists in unison. Every hand was streaked with red. The Watcher turned away from them, heading for the steps.

Raine trembled.

"Surrender your weapons, or it will kill you," I said.

The monster reached the steps. It looked at me, and I held out my hand. A droplet of blood glimmered on the edge of my finger. It turned away from me and headed for Raine.

"Decide quickly," I shouted.

The Watcher roared, and the others on the wall echoed it. A chorus of snarls filled the air as more creatures surged from the forest. More than a dozen Watchers. Among them walked my sister.

Raine grabbed the rifle from the nearest soldier's hands and aimed it straight at my heart. "Never," he snarled.

I jumped back as his finger squeezed the trigger. Pain blossomed in my arm, and I fell to my knees. Through a haze of agony, I saw the Watcher bound forward and snatch him up in a single swoop of its jaws. Raine screamed. I turned my head away.

The other soldiers dropped their weapons and threw up their arms in surrender.

It was over.

~

Our people shed their disguises and confiscated the soldiers' weapons. They bound the soldiers' hands and then locked them all in their own prison cells—the very cell block from which I'd rescued my sister—both to contain them and to protect them from being mauled by the Watchers that had settled into an agitated crouch beside the village gates.

I remained on the steps of the Assembly Hall while Adam bound up my injured arm.

"It only grazed you," he said, dabbing the wound with brandy and then binding it with a clean rag. "Does it hurt?"

"Like fire," I muttered, giving him a shaky smile.

He helped me up and gave me a gulp of the brandy for the pain, and then together we climbed the steps to meet the Mayor. He'd sunk down onto the top stair.

"I can't believe I did that," he murmured, looking up at me. His face was ashen. "Incredible. Look at them. I'd never seen one before, and now—" He gestured at the Watchers by the gate. Their now-golden eyes were watchful as they tracked his movements. "When Jullia Dyer came to me telling me that Bluewing had a serum that would inoculate us against the Watchers and allow us to use them in the liberation, I thought she was mad," the Mayor said. "But it worked." He gazed down at his hand, where a single trickle of blood marred his skin. He fingered it with reverence. "It worked," he repeated.

Adam and I said nothing, but we understood his relief. We'd spent many sleepless nights agonizing over the possibility that something would go wrong, that our desperate gamble would fail.

"What now?" The Mayor asked. "Will you stay or go? Are you even from the Frost, either of you?"

Adam reached up and pulled off his mask.

The Mayor jerked in astonishment. "Adam Brewer—but you were arrested...you were in an Aeralian prison..."

"Bluewing brought me back," he said, with a faint smile.

The Mayor's eyes slid to me. I undid my mask as well. I heard ripples of surprise from the other Blackcoats in the square behind me.

"Lia Weaver." The Mayor shook his head. "We thought you were dead."

"Not dead," I said. "Not yet."

Adam and I withdrew to speak privately.

"How long do we keep the Watchers here?" I asked him.

"We'll march the Farthers across the river before nightfall. We'll need the Watchers to remain until then."

We stood shoulder to shoulder, he and I, and my heart swelled as I looked at my village, with its wind-weathered stone and broken streets of cobblestone and the sea of cloaks that milled before us. Iceliss.

It was good to be home again.

TWENTY-FIVE

AFTER THE FARTHER soldiers had been carted across the river in their own wagons and deposited on the far shore with only potatoes to feed them on their journey to Aeralis, we watched them flee, pale and shaken, sneaking glances back at us and the monsters with glowing eyes that lurked behind us. I knew this was a story those soldiers would tell their grandchildren one day—how they saw the fabled beasts come from the forest, and how their eyes were the color of blood and scarlet, and how the monsters did not attack the Frost dwellers.

And I knew a legend would be born from it, a legend that might keep us safe again.

"It's not over quite yet," Adam reminded me as we took the path toward the now-useless Cages that stood in the snow, a grim testament to the scarring of our world by the Aeralian occupation. "Korr will be back, wanting payment for his part in this. Are you going to give it to him?"

"I don't know," I admitted. "I don't trust him...but Ann does, and he did do what he promised. What does the Trio think?"

"I will contact them tonight with the news of our victory, and Korr's bargain. I will defer to their judgment on the matter, and so should you."

The oath I'd sworn to the Thorns seemed too long ago now, faded and irrelevant in light of everything we'd struggled to accomplish since. I stopped and turned to him. "Will they join him? Will the Thorns support his fight against the dictator?"

"Perhaps," Adam said, in his cryptic way.

When I gave him a look, he only smiled.

The Watchers did not follow us when we reached the Cages. They turned away from the stream of people and headed for the trees. Among them I saw a scrape of pale blue and a flutter of light brown hair. Ivy.

Part of me wanted to call her back, but I didn't.

I thought of Jonn. He'd refused to accompany us, and I understood. Seeing the Watchers was still too painful for him. We'd left him to wait in my family's farmhouse alone. And Gabe... I hadn't seen him since the victory in the square, or Claire for that matter. Neither of them had accompanied us to see the Farthers across the river.

Music trickled through the darkness, growing stronger as we reached the village and entered the streets. Night was falling, and people had lit bonfires in the middle of the cobblestoned roads. Men and women danced, and children ran and laughed and clapped their hands. Everything was bathed in firelight, transforming the sad shell of our village into something infused with magic. Someone threw a log on one of the fires, and a flood of sparks flew into the darkening sky. An emotion I couldn't name swelled in me, squeezing my throat.

Ann found me amid the throng of reveling villagers. "I've been looking for you," she shouted over the music and laughter. "My father wants to speak with you. With both of you," she said, nodding at Adam.

~

"I am stepping down as Mayor," he announced to the small circle of people who'd gathered inside the

Assembly Hall. "It will be announced tomorrow, but I wanted you to know tonight."

The flicker of candlelight danced over the faces of his audience, revealing expressions of shock, dismay, and relief. Even I was surprised. He was willingly abdicating? How would this change the system, the village, everything?

"How is such a thing possible? You are Mayor," someone protested. "It is your position, your name."

"And I've been a horrible one. The people have no faith in me anymore, and I don't blame them for it. So perhaps it's time for a new Mayor."

A new Mayor. Whispers fluttered in the silence that followed that statement. I met Adam's eyes, and words passed unspoken between us. The right choice could redefine everything about our way of life here. And the wrong choice...well.

I supposed we'd find out what everyone thought about this tomorrow.

~

I went alone on horseback to fetch my brother. The sight of the farm made my eyes prickle as I reached the top of the hill, and I dismounted and stood for a moment, just taking it in. It had only been a few months since we'd fled from this place, but the time between felt like years. So much had changed. So much was gone, and what was left had been rearranged and reassembled into something new and strange.

I went inside and found Jonn at his old table, his elbows braced on the wood and his head in his hands. He didn't look up as I entered.

"Is it done?" His voice was muffled.

"It's done. They're all gone across the river, and I don't think they're coming back."

He sighed, and I heard a million words of sorrow and longing in the sound.

"Come with me, brother. Let's go back to the village. They're celebrating."

He shook his head. "I'm going to stay here."

"You're not. You're coming back with me."

He didn't reply.

He'd made a fire, and I went to extinguish the coals. Something was burning amid the logs—a box. I crouched down and squinted to see it better. "Jonn, this is the package I brought you from Borde."

"Yes," he muttered.

"You're burning it?"

"I don't need it now."

Curiosity stirred in me. I leaned forward, but I couldn't see what had been inside. Flames had consumed everything but the metal container, which glowed with heat.

"Jonn..." After all I'd gone through to get it, he was simply burning it?

"Forget it," he snapped, and I fell silent. Did this have something to do with Everiss?

"Let's go," I said.

"No. Leave me here. I want to be alone."

He made a wheezing sound that might have been a sob, and then he was silent. I waited by the fire. After a long while, he slumped forward in sheer exhaustion, asleep.

I struggled to get him onto the horse alone, and I took him with me back to Iceliss. He didn't stir the entire way there.

~

The villagers gathered in the Assembly Hall the next morning at the Mayor's request. Curious murmurs thickened the air, and nervous energy twisted in my stomach. I sat with Ann on one side of me and a pale-looking Jonn on the other. I hadn't seen Adam since the night before. I still hadn't seen Gabe, either. I twisted in my seat, looking for them among the throng behind us.

The Mayor stepped onto the dais at the front of the hall and held up his hands for order. He looked so different from his former self. The skin hung from his bones and the places beneath his eyes were hollow now. His hair was grayer.

"Please," he said loudly, and his voice carried through the room.

The talking quieted, and every villager leaned forward in his or her seat. Faces were knit with a mixture of happiness and suspicion, confusion and anger. The last several times he'd addressed us in this hall, it had not gone well.

"Today, I stand before you a broken man," the Mayor began. "I almost lost my beloved daughter. I did lose my pride, my morals, and your trust."

The room waited. I held my breath.

"So, for the crimes I have committed against this village and my people, I am resigning my position as Mayor."

Voices erupted in confused chatter, and he held up his hands again for silence.

"What's going to happen to the village?" someone shouted.

"The council of Elders will choose the new—"

"Why not let the people choose?" a voice called out from the back.

I turned in my seat along with the entire hall to see Gabe standing in the doorway, outlined by light, his hair blown by wind and his cheeks reddened from the cold. My heart thudded.

"I..." the Mayor began.

"Yes, why not?" This time it was my sister who spoke up. She jumped from her seat to face the room.

"Ivy," I said in a harsh whisper. "What are you doing?"

Gabe strode down the center aisle until he'd reached the front of the room. "Where were the Elders when the Farthers took over this village? Where were they when we were all starving?"

"Excuse me," the Mayor managed. "But who are you?"

"My name is Gabe, and I'm a member of the group that liberated this village yesterday. And no, it isn't my village, but I can see your problems all the same. You have too much secrecy. Too much unbalanced power. More than half this village has no say, no vote, and all because of their family name."

Ann leaped from her seat and approached the dais. "Gabe has a good point," she said. "Besides, half the Elders are dead or imprisoned. Raine ground our old system to bits beneath his boots, and maybe this time, when we're putting everything back together, we should build it a new way."

"How?" someone asked from the back. Heads nodded.

"We'll have an election," she said. "We'll choose a new Mayor, all of us." Her gaze rested on me, and I shook my head vigorously. Her gaze slid on to rest beside me.

"I nominate Jonn Weaver for the position of Mayor of Iceliss. He planned most of the revolution yesterday. He's a hard worker, a loyal brother, and a good friend."

249

Jonn's expression was unreadable, but I could see shock in the way his eyes widened ever so slightly. He lowered his head as the air around him ignited with whispers.

Gabe left the front of the room. As he passed us, he leaned down and murmured in my ear, "I would like to speak with you before I leave."

Before I leave.

The words struck me through the heart like an arrow. I rose to my feet and followed him out of the hall, but when I'd reached the outside, he'd already vanished.

Adam found me standing on the steps, staring at the sky.

"Where've you been?" I asked.

"The forest," he said. "Contacting the Trio." He went to the door of the Assembly Hall and listened. "They're deliberating about a new Mayor," he said. "I don't think you want to miss it."

"I don't," I said, turning to go back inside.

But he stopped me with a gentle hand. "Gabe?" he asked.

"He's leaving."

Adam's expression was a question. "And you?"

Pain splintered in my chest. I'd thought about this, and I'd come to a decision. Adam's eyes were watchful as they met mine. He waited for me to speak.

I slipped my hand into his. "Let's go back inside."

~

Deliberations lasted for most of the day, and by the time the sun set, we had six nominations for a new Mayor, and tenuous discussions about how to go about setting up a method of choosing him or her. I continued to look for Gabe, but he was nowhere to be found. Adam sensed my distress. He put a hand over mine, and that calmed me a little.

When darkness had gathered, I left the hall again and went out onto the steps. Stars glittered overhead, and the night air was like ice. My breath made a cloud as I exhaled. To my left, a shadow stirred from beside the wall, and I realized it was Gabe. He wore a cloak and carried a sack over one shoulder.

"I've been looking for you—" I began.

"Come with me." He stepped toward me until he was only inches away. His eyes held mine, and the intensity in his gaze burned me to my core.

"Come where? Why are you going?"

"Oh, don't pretend I can stay here. The Farthers are gone, Lia. You and the others have been welcomed back with open arms. I'm an outsider now, just as I was before."

"The other fugitives—"

"Most of the others are going with me, too."

I didn't know what to say.

"Come with me," he repeated.

"You're returning to Aeralis?"

"Not just that," he said. "I'm joining my brother. We're going to overthrow the Aeralian dictator. We're going to take back our nation."

Join Korr? "Why the sudden change of heart?"

Only then did I notice Claire, leaning against the wall of the Assembly Hall, her arms crossed beneath her cloak. She said nothing.

"He helped us, didn't he? He didn't betray us. He came here to look for me."

"But it's Korr."

Gabe didn't respond to that. "I want you to come with me," he said again. "You've proven yourself capable when it comes to revolutions. We could use you."

251

I flinched at the coldness of the request. *We could use you.* Was that all this was about? Utility?

"I'm not Aeralian," I said.

"No," he said, "But you'd be welcome among us. And you might find that the Frost seems very small when all is said and done."

"I can't leave now."

"Then don't. Think about it. I'll be back to get the PLD you promised my brother."

He stepped forward and kissed me; it was a goodbye and a promise.

I reached for him, but my hands stopped short. He pulled back and looked at me. We didn't say anything.

Gabe turned and vanished with Claire into the darkness, and I was alone on the front steps of the Assembly Hall, my lips still tingling from his kiss and my mind spinning from his words.

"Lia!"

Footsteps rang out behind me, and I turned just as Ivy burst through the Assembly Hall door.

"Come quickly," she gasped. "Jonn's just collapsed."

"A seizure?" I was already moving.

"No," she panted. "Adam says he thinks it's the Sickness!"

Look for Book 5 in The Frost Chronicles, *Aeralis*, coming summer 2013!

ACKNOWLEDGEMENTS

Scott, for being my strongest supporter, my most faithful friend, the best husband I could ever imagine, and the kindest person I know. Thank you for always encouraging me. Thank you for everything you do for me and my writing career.

My family, for being so enthusiastic and supportive of my career. You guys are awesome, and I love you all very much.

My mother-in-law, for staying up super-late to read *Weavers*.

Dani H. Crabtree, for being such an awesome editor and for making time for my crazy and last-minute schedule. Thank you for your insightful comments, creative direction, and kick-butt work.

My readers, for passionately loving the world of the Frost and all the characters who inhabit it. Thank you for messaging and emailing me about my books. Your enthusiasm is better writing fuel than chocolate pie, and that's saying a lot.

ABOUT THE AUTHOR

Kate Avery Ellison lives in Atlanta, Georgia, with her husband and two spoiled (but extremely lovable) cats. She loves dark chocolate, fairy tale retellings, and love stories with witty banter and sizzling, unspoken feelings. When she isn't working on her next writing project, she can be found reading, watching one of her favorite TV shows, working on an endless list of DIY household projects, or hanging out with friends.

You can find more information about Kate Avery Ellison's books and other upcoming projects online at http://thesouthernscrawl.blogspot.com/.

CPSIA information can be obtained
at www.ICGtesting.com
Printed in the USA
LVHW100245260822
726925LV00011B/64